Theron Clark Crawford

A Man and his Soul

An Occult Romance of Washington Life

Theron Clark Crawford

A Man and his Soul
An Occult Romance of Washington Life

ISBN/EAN: 9783337347482

Printed in Europe, USA, Canada, Australia, Japan

Cover: Foto ©Andreas Hilbeck / pixelio.de

More available books at **www.hansebooks.com**

A · Man · and · His · Soul

AN OCCULT ROMANCE OF WASHINGTON LIFE

BY

T. C. CRAWFORD

AUTHOR OF "SENATOR STANLEY'S STORY," "THE DISAPPEARANCE SYNDICATE," "ENGLISH LIFE
THROUGH YANKEE EYES," "AMERICAN VENDETTA," "LIFE OF
JAMES G. BLAINE," ETC., ETC.

NEW YORK:

CHARLES B. REED, PUBLISHER,

164, 166 & 168 FULTON ST.

———

1894.

A Man and His Soul.

CONTENTS.

CONTENTS.

CHAPTER I.

WHERE I MADE THE ACQUAINTANCE OF A PERFECTLY HAPPY MAN.

After years of absence from my former home in Washington, I found great pleasure in returning for another winter to the National Capital. Yet, after a time, I found the renewing of experience a dull method of passing the time. There was, at first, but little going on of exceptional interest. In society there were no great scandals, nor transcendent beauties, discovered. In politics, small things and small men, according to the newspapers, filled the horizon. I, who had, formerly, for years, filled the post of a special correspondent in Washington, was obliged to confess that if I were now to begin life as a newspaper observer at the Capital, I could not find enough to do, to make myself worthy of employment.

But, I had not been long in Washington, upon the occasion of my last visit, before I met Captain Arthur Harcourt, and after that I did not have a dull moment. He gave a shake to the hour-glass of time for me, and the sands, which had been creeping along at so slow a pace, now moved with the swiftest possible motion. We measure time by our endurance or enjoyment of it. Measured by my new sensations, a day soon 'counted as nothing.

Pardon my extravagance. I will try and make it plain why Captain Harcourt proved so interesting to a correspondent, who had now reached middle life and who had seen the most notable events of modern history in the last quarter of the century, both in the old world as well as the new.

I made Captain Harcourt's acquaintance at the Arlington Hotel, where I was living. He was also a guest in the same house. I first saw him in the open and hospitable white marble-floored office of this hotel. Under the flashing lights of this high-ceilinged room, in front of its open fires, are to be found, during the winter evenings, some of the most notable people in Washington. Seated in a broad-armed easy chair, with a cigar, I often spent an hour after dinner glancing at the moving figures in this Washington world, which becomes so active and alert when evening arrives. From the central seat, which was my favorite one, I could command many points of advantage. Through the broad windows at the left, under the striped-canvas awning, there were continually appearing and disappearing carriages, occupied by ladies resplendent in the brilliancy of evening toilettes. The arrival and departure of these guests, coming or going from some one of the many receptions of the night, during the busy season, the slamming of carriage doors, the shuffling of the feet of the colored servants about the corridors, where they moved about happy as children, the sharp clang of the bell of the clerk in the hotel office, the strains of music from an orchestral band in attendance upon a private dinner in some one of the great drawing-rooms of the first floor, combined with the hum of voices of people moving about, made up a fascinating medley of action and sound. The arrival of guests before the hotel register was also a constant subject of comment from the groups seated about the office, as they recognized this or that prominent man among the late comers. Among those who were seated around the open, blazing fires were occasional Justices of the Supreme Court, numerous members of Congress, a rare United States Senator and, sometimes, a democratic member of the President's Cabinet. But those who had offices to bestow were not allowed to sit at their ease long, as those who beg for place and official favors came in hungry and genteel-shabby groups, patrolling every nook of the hotel lobby, seeking some high official to torment with impossible demands.

Every night, after my arrival, I observed that one of the guests of the hotel came, after his dinner, always to the same seat, and that he remained in it during the greater part of the evening. He did not appear to have any acquaintance with any other of the guests of the hotel, and yet he did not give me the impression of being reserved or cold. I was first attracted to him by his air of perfect tranquility, and by the exquisite courtesy and simplicity of his manners. He was tall and spare of figure. His color was that of high health; of one accustomed to much outdoor life. His features were irregular and far from handsome; but, yet, his expression of kindness and content awakened from the first my interest and then my envy. I watched him carefully, day by day, to see some shadow upon this supremely contented face; but its expression, while constantly changing, never varied its key. Evidently here was a man who was contented, and, yet, what were his resources for such happiness? I watched him for several days before I sought to speak to him. No one could live more simply than he. He came to the dining-room, only to order the simplest of foods. Fruit in abundance was heaped up before him, when he came to the table, almost to the exclusion of other things. He rarely drank wine, and then in the most moderate quantities.

The waiters, the black children of Washington, who are so keen to detect kind hearts, and who prize gentle words above bribes of silver, were devoted to Captain Harcourt.

Inquiry at the office concerning him disclosed but little. He was a former officer of the Navy, who had resigned a number of years ago, so many that, now, since his return to Washington, he found few who knew him or who remembered him in the past. He appeared to have money, at least for his modest wishes. He lived quietly, went out but little, never complained, paid his bills promptly and never objected to the charges for extras. "A model guest; I would to God we had more like him," said the pale-faced clerk, looking me firmly in the eye, as he answered my questions. If I had not been an old correspondent, he probably would have answered none of my questions; for, in this old-fashioned hotel, the aristocratic proprietor was fond of furnishing privacy to his guests with the other comforts of his hospitable house. I remembered, as the clerk gazed so firmly at me, that I had that morning disputed a mysterious extra in my weekly bill; and had I not, through years of acquaintance, earned the right to trifle occasionally with the management? Yet, this pointed reference to the magnificent virtue of Captain Harcourt in this regard, warned me that even my old position in the house did not warrant me in taking too serious a liberty with the business management, or to suppose, for one instant, that it could be possible for it to err.

I do not think I should have taken the trouble to become acquainted with Captain Harcourt if it had not been for his expression of unalloyed content. If it had been stupid content, such as is found sometimes upon the face of the human animal—who ruminates as he digests some skillfully-prepared dinner, while he contemplates with rapture his well-groomed and well-housed condition—I should not have given him a second thought. No; his content appeared to me to be an intellectual one. His face bore the look of a man thoroughly at peace with himself. There are not so many faces of this kind in the world that I, a professional observer of men, could afford to pass Captain Harcourt by.

At that time, I was dull and thoroughly discontented with myself. I had good health, and so I was saved from being a cynic; but there was, gradually, beginning to steal over me the sensation of weariness and discouragement, which are the natural heritages of life when the illusions of youth are gone and the grim realities of old age begin to appear through the misty clouds of the future. The fact that Captain Harcourt, who was fifty years of age, and at least ten years older than I, had so conclusively settled one of the greatest problems of life, by finding, apparently, a pure and perfect contentment, based upon something higher than mere physical satisfaction, stimulated my curiosity to the highest degree.

What was this source of interior content? The Captain was the most inactive of men. His eyes, a deep steely blue, glowed with soft fire, but, yet, had a curiously wide-awake look. I found, so often, the Captain's face, as we sat in the hotel lobby in the evening, changing with varying expressions of interest and enjoyment, that I often caught myself looking here and there to see what could so interest this quiet, unassuming gentleman, who smoked his mild Oriental cigarettes with such a careless grace, as if the beauty of the forms of the spiral smoke, ascending above his head, interested and touched his eye more keenly than the taste of the tobacco did his palate.

One evening, I could no longer contain my curiosity. I spoke to Captain Harcourt, and you may trust an old correspondent for the fact that my advance upon his privacy was made upon the most artistic and approved lines. Yet, I might have spared myself my artful manœuvres.

He interposed not the slightest obstacle in the way of reserve to my advances. Like a true man of the world he adjusted himself to my wishes and, after a moment of careless talk about nothing, he surprised me by saying: " I have been expecting you to speak to me all the evening."

" Did I watch you so closely as all that ? "

" Oh, no ; I was conscious that you were, to a certain extent, interested in my individuality. I have piqued your intellectual curiosity. You are the first person in Washington who has taken the trouble to observe me at all."

" I trust, in no disagreeable sense ? "

" Oh, not at all. It is a compliment to me as the case stands."

The conversation that followed was, for a time, upon casual topics. The quiet, easy, tranquil air of Captain Harcourt so impressed me that, as a prelude to the natural inquiries of the opening of an acquaintance between strangers, I handed him my card. In return he gave me his :

Mr. Arthur Harcourt.

ISLAND OF NOLOS.

As I looked at his card, I said : " Forgive me ; but where is the Island of Nolos ? "

" Few people know where it is, or have even heard of it," said Captain Harcourt, as he was called in the official atmosphere of Washington, where a title once given is never dropped. " It is a very small place.

It is in South African waters. It is about eighty
miles from the sea-coast of Mashonaland. The island
contains not over one thousand acres. I own half of it.
The other half is owned by an English friend of mine.
The island makes for us two very snug coffee plantations. We live there alone the greater part of the
year."

"But how do you pass the time ? Are you wholly
alone ; that is, without family ? "

"We are both bachelors. We have negro servants
to attend to the plantations. The climate is perfect
and is rarely hot or cold. We have all the publications of interest from the capitals of the world sent to
us, and, when we get tired, we run out into the world
for a little change. But we do not go very often. My
present outward visit is the first one of long duration
since going to the island. Now, I shall spend at least
the winter here, and, before going back, shall remain
one season at London and Paris."

"But how did you, an American naval officer, come
to establish a house upon an island in such far-away
waters? You do not have the air of a hermit or of a
recluse who would seek to shun the world."

"The explanation is simple enough. Ten years ago
I was retired from the Navy on account of weak lungs
and consequent ill health. Six months after my retirement, my physician, who examined me, told me that, at
best, I did not have more than half a year to live. The
period might be extended to a year if I could find
some gentle, equable climate, free from cold and damp-
ness, where I could live wholly out of doors. It was

then that I thought with pleasure of the air of the high table-lands of South Africa, where I had once, upon a furlough, gone on a hunting expedition. I sold what little property I had; and, as I had no near family ties of any kind, went away to die alone, in the most peaceful and least painful way possible. On my way out to South Africa, from London, I became acquainted with Doctor Maurice Longman. He was the owner of the Island of Nolos, where he spent the greater part of his time in study. He said to me that he could not promise me a positive return to health; but upon this peaceful island, with his care, he felt sure that I would find my life greatly prolonged. Like the prisoner upon his way to execution, I hailed his offer in the light of a reprieve. Need I say that this chance encounter proved to be one of the most fortunate of my life? Through Doctor Longman and his teachings I regained, wholly, my health; and found a contentment so perfect that no one could believe without understanding, fully, its basis. In other words, I have to-day perfect health and perfect happiness."

" If what you say is true, you are the richest man in the world. The perfectly happy man does not exist, not even in legend nor story."

" Yet, you must believe me when I tell you I am such a man."

" But, how can it be proved. It would not be difficult to allege and to sustain that any man who is contented with life as it is now lived, is either a fool or an amiable lunatic. Now, you do not have the air of being either; yet, when you assert that you are perfectly happy, my only refuge is to disbelieve what you say, in as polite a fashion as it is possible to express incredulity."

"I not only assert that I am perfectly happy, but I desire to strengthen and broaden the declaration: I hold in my hands perfect happiness. No human power could augment or decrease this happiness. Neither is it probable, although possible, that this condition of mine will change."

"You have, then, everything you desire or may wish to have?"

"Everything!"

"Oh, wonderful man, will you give me, some day, when you know me better, your recipe for perfect happiness?"

"Yes; I will."

"Can you give it to me here, or must I go to the Island of Nolos to undergo a novitiate? In the wonderful stories I have read of the unattainable, the candidates are made to undergo preliminary trials and purifications."

The Captain smiled and lazily followed, with supremely contented eyes, a shadowy, blue cloud, as he said : "A visit to the Island of Nolos will not be absolutely necessary, although you may find it agreeable and desirable to go there some day. Before I leave Washington, I will try and teach you the certain road to happiness. But there is no hurry; you must first be convinced that I am happy. If I cannot make you see that, there will be a difficulty about your arriving at the second stage."

I must confess that I was, in a measure, discouraged at this reply. The Captain's attitude was one I could not dispute. If he was the sole and undisturbed owner of unalloyed happiness, I had no right to any special favor from him; neither was I then inclined to attach too much importance to the conversation. It was simply interesting. There was a charm about Captain Harcourt, however, which made him a most agreeable companion.

I might have talked more with him, upon the evening of my first acquaintance with him, had it not been for an interruption. Every special correspondent at Washington has an army of cranky followers, who regard his newspaper as the vehicle of woe and retribution for the wicked officials of the National Capitol. These reformers lay in wait for the writers of the press, and breathe forth tales of dishonesty and corruption that chill with horror the blood of youth; but I am a veteran of some years of this kind of recital, and so I was not at all pleased when Professor Optics, a reformer, who believed everybody but himself was a villain of dark degree, now bore down upon me for a brief chat of fifteen hours upon the hideous dishonesty of modern official life.

I compromised with the professor for forty-seven cents. He was always borrowing such absurd sums; and, with his promise to return the same at twenty-seven minutes after three, in the afternoon, on the 14th of the following month, I finally escaped him, and went out to the reception given that evening by the wife of a popular senator, and so saw no more of Captain Arthur Harcourt until nearly the same hour, just after the late dinner of next day.

CHAPTER II.

CAPTAIN HARCOURT AND I BECAME FRIENDS.

The next evening, when I took my seat by the side of Captain Harcourt, it seemed as if we were already friends. I do not make friends readily. My profession had taught me the art of easily making acquaintances; but friends were rarely found, and, to tell the truth, but casually sought. I had always held that one or, perhaps, two friends exhausted one's strength in that direction; for I construed friendship as something quite as obligatory and sacred as the marriage contract itself.

Yet, when I once more engaged in conversation with Captain Harcourt, I had the interior conviction that this man and I were to become intimate. He had, first, for me, the interest of an engaging individuality; then, that sixth sense of a newspaper correspondent, which we read so much about in the entrancing hand-books of journalism, made easy in ten lessons, told me so. I felt that the Captain had an interesting and odd story to tell. And who loves an odd story more than a professional writer, and who enjoys such a story more than a veteran correspondent, who is more pleased with the reserve of its owner than if he had, at the outset, frankly told him his history and of how he had arrived where no man had ever before arrived,—at the plane of perfect happiness?

How many times did I seek to test the correctness of the Captain's assertion! As we talked, running around the world for topics, I found, always, the note of the clear observer, and the tone of an unprejudiced judgment. Such clearness, such correctness, such justice and breadth of view, would have made him prominent at once in any intellectual gathering. His observations, too, were always clothed in simple language.

During the preliminaries of our acquaintance, which bid fair to ripen into friendship, there was but little, if any, reference to the extraordinary assertion made by the Captain upon the evening we first met. Yet, I could but note the atmosphere of peaceful content about the man. Children and the negro servants all turned towards him instinctively, and I soon found that I was never more contented and at ease, than when I was seated by his side, in the hotel lobby, with the ever-changing groups round about us.

There was an engaging air of innocent mystery about the Captain that constantly filled my mind with interest. I longed for some severe trial, some emotional shock, which should put to the test his absurd claim of perfect happiness. The word content was not enough for him. He had used the word happiness; and here he was, alone, with almost no tie between him and the circling humanities around him, a citizen of Nolos, living, without any apparent object in life, the life of a man who seemed to do nothing, yet, whose face was not that of a sluggard, and whose eyes showed noble purpose, even, in the soft light of their perfect content. It was rather trying—this perfect satisfaction with life. It was a new experience to me to meet a happy man. I had always heard that he did not exist. It had been my fortune, during twenty years of active work as a special correspondent, to meet the great and successful in every city of note in the world. Yet, whether presidents of republics, royalties, diplomats, statesmen, artists or financiers, over all hovered some black shadow of care. I had never before seen a man, however rich in money, fame or honor, who had reached the plane of ordinary content. There was always some hopeless Beyond that beckoned him on, and poisoned the pleasure of the success obtained.

I did not, at first, believe too much in Captain Harcourt's happiness. I longed to see it put to some proof. The placid and tranquil life of a man of leisure, in a fashionable hotel at the heighth of the Washington season, was no place for tests ; but I was soon to see him tried, and to learn, at first, slowly, and at last, suddenly, some of the mighty reasons for this change in the type of the sorrowful human race, which carries, with curses or sullen patience, according to the temperament, the heavy burden of ordinary life.

One night, at the end of about a week of our acquaintance, I saw the character of the Captain tested in a slight trial, which gave me a brief insight into his philosophy. I am of a nature that cannot bear the sight of pain or suffering in others without a sharp pang. Selfish injustice stirs the very blood of my heart, as the bugle note inflames the war horse with the fire of battle.

If I could hold all the injustice in this world once in my hand, and crush it, I believe I could die happy.

Upon this particular night, when I was to learn whether this perfect happiness had for its basis a perfect selfishness, which I suspected, there came into the group about the open fire a statesman, long famed, in the House, for his cynical ability, his wit, his readiness in debate and his colossal vanity, which made him more cruel and ungrateful than a peacock.

I well remember the picture the statesman made; for, inconsequential as he was at times, he yet had been a potent influence in the shaping of the legislation of the war, and in the reconstruction laws which followed. His spare, slight figure was clothed in evening dress, over which he wore a long fur-lined overcoat, which descended nearly to his heels. His dark, olive-tinted, hard-lined face was shadowed by a long mustache and short beard. A dark evening hat was cocked rakishly over one ear. A dark perfecto cigar was held tightly in one corner of his grinning mouth. He was just in from a jolly dinner. He was flushed with good cheer and excitement. About him were grouped a gathering of local followers, who greeted their member's cynical witticisms with loud laughter that echoed through the corridors, and started every ebony face among the servants grinning with contagious sympathy. Stimulated by the laughter of his satellites, and warmed by the atmosphere, the diminutive statesman was at his best. The voice that had resounded through the hall of the House of Representatives in witty and rasping speech, cruelly tearing at the foibles of the opposition, was now low-toned and honey-tongued. One story followed another with the rapidity of delivery of a consummate artist, when, suddenly, there was a break in the sound of revelry.

I turned to see the cause of this sudden change. It was occasioned by the presence of an humble-mannered old man, with white, silky hair, falling in long masses from his battered and worn hat. His garments were shabby, and ill fitted to protect his trembling limbs from the bleak cold of the winter night, from which the old man had just entered. He had passed through the groups of the stalwart colored porters, who filled the hall, without opposition. The fact that he was a gentleman, and in keen distress, made him an object of sympathy for these black servants, the only really kind-hearted servants in the world ; and so this old man, the representative of poverty and suffering, had been able to enter through the brilliant halls, and reach the jovial group in front of the sparkling fire, which flashed its long, flaming smiles of welcome upon the just and unjust as they came before it.

It was an ill-selected moment for the unfortunate man to make his appeal for aid to the witty statesman, who was the centre of the admiring group already described. He actually broke in upon one of his most admirable stories without waiting for its artistic climax.

With a voice nearly broken with emotion, the trembling man said : "Oh, honored sir, a word with you !"

The statesman turned impatiently. "Let it be a short one. Who let you in here, anyway, to annoy gentlemen ?"

" You know me, sir."

" I should think I did. You worried my life half out of me last year, until I got your daughter a place in the Department for the Gathering of Useless Information. You wrote me yesterday that she had been discharged, and that you would starve unless something was done. Now, I tell you, I won't do anything more for you. Get out !"

" But my daughter——"

" Let her learn how to keep a place next time."

" But, sir, she resented the insults of her Chief of Bureau and——"

" Oh, yes ; I know that old story. There is no variety in it. How can a woman expect to keep a place in Washington, and have all the deference shown her that one would pay a woman in society?"

" It is not that, sir ; she should have the respect paid an honest woman."

" Well, I don't propose to discuss it. I won't do anything more. I don't care whether your daughter is respectable or not. She had a place. If she was not smart enough to keep it, that is her lookout."

" But do not turn me away. Remember the past."

At this daring allusion to some past service, the statesman became livid with passion and shook his fist in the face of the old man, and called to the servants to remove the old beggar.

But not a black boy moved. I was now up, erect, aflame with indignation. Captain Harcourt gently pressed me by the arm, and we followed the old man out without attracting notice. I was choked with my emotion; the Captain was as calm and serene as ever. But his face wore a look of almost divine pity and gentleness that calmed my rage. I forgave him, at last, his serenity, and no longer assumed that it was based upon selfishness.

We caught up with the old man just outside the hotel and soon learned his sorrowful story. Once he had been a rich and prosperous merchant, and had furnished the money that started the statesman at the beginning of his political career. No wonder the latter hated his former benefactor! This sad, old man found in us two friends; and, the next morning, I had the pleasure of learning that, sometimes, a special correspondent at Washington has his day of influence. When I told the story of the indignity, to the member of the Cabinet who presided over the department in question, he made, apparently, a mental calculation as to the effect of such a story, printed in a prominent New York newspaper; and then decided, in the most amiable fashion, to restore the young lady to her post of duty, with a well-worded apology for the injustice done. The offending Chief of Bureau was not discharged. I knew my Washington too well to expect that. He was simply transferred to another post of duty. But this incident greatly endeared Captain Harcourt to me, so heartily did he support me in this attempt to right one of the lesser acts of injustice of this greatly overgoverned National Capital.

CHAPTER III.

THE AMBASSADOR FROM THE ISLAND OF NOLOS.

I now observed that Captain Harcourt was ever
open to pity, and was always ready to right injustice.
But there was always this difference : with him there was
no excessive emotion or agitation. He wished to restore
the rights of the wronged ; but he never expressed any
indignation, or sought, by word or threat, to remotely
suggest a punishment for the offenders. Yet, I would
not have you think that we, at this time, discussed any
such grave questions as the justice and injustice of
modern life. No ; the impression I formed was from
the slight experiences I had with him in the consideration of certain individual cases. For, at Washington, the
special correspondent, if he does his duty, is the modern knight errant. To him come nearly all the people
who suffer from official injustice. To be sure, they
often come in company with the malicious and the
mischief-loving ; but the sincere writer soon learns to
discriminate, and, upon certain very rare occasions,
mounted upon the back of his newspaper, with his
goose quill couched as a lance, he has been fortunate
enough to win a victory over some official who has
done a wrong, before the latter has been able to muster
the influence required to head him off, by orders direct
from the publication headquarters.

Yet, it was a long time before the Captain could be prevailed upon to talk about himself. After the first few evenings, I met him constantly. I could not even explain to myself my very great interest in him. Very soon I acquired the habit of dropping into his rooms in the morning, and, almost before I knew it, I was spending the greater part of my waking moments with him. He was so very gentle, so very much at his ease, and so thoroughly at home upon all subjects. My interest, however, was something more than a mere intellectual one. I soon began to feel for him a real affection ; and I assure you that it has not been my habit, during the later years of my life, to find myself very sensitive in this direction.

One night, when I was in his room, a card came up for me from the office below. It was the card of a valiant old friend of mine, who had, for twenty years, sought vainly to obtain justice from the Government of the United States. He was one of those unfortunates who had a claim against the Government, and who possessed neither money nor friends for its prosecution.

I was going down to see him, when the Captain asked me to have him come up to his room, where we were. I shall never forget the look on his face, as my friend, the claimant, Hugh McGregor, stood with his back to the fire-place and told, in a succinct and manly way, the history of the progress he had made with Congress that winter. It was almost pitiable to look at his splendid, sturdy courage, and to feel that so much physical vitality, so much indomitable energy, so much loyal courage, such an unyielding will, and such unchangeable cheerfulness should have been wasted upon the hopeless task of compelling the Government of the United States to do its duty toward a private debtor. His twenty years of defeat had not yet taken the light from his splendid blue-gray eyes; notwithstanding his sixty years of age, the ruddy color of health was to be seen in his cheeks, and, even now, the silver had hardly begun to appear in his dark-brown hair. His modest dress was a model of neatness. I do not propose, here, to recapitulate his story, because the world knows the pitiable fate of a claimant in Washington. But, as he talked, I thought that I saw Captain Harcourt looking, all the time, behind him, during his discourse. I knew that he was kind-hearted. I was confident that he would believe in the man, because he was my friend; but, at no time, during his talk, did his eyes for more than one moment rest upon his face, even when McGregor bowed himself out.

This was a point which I put down in my private note-book; for it was understood between us that, at the proper time, my friend would give me full explanation of what I had thought mysterious in his assertions, or in his conduct.

First, I tested his sympathy, by telling him briefly the story of McGregor, who had been wronged out of a great property by a rich corporation, and whose alleged rights came to them through a wrong assumption of authority upon the part of the United States Government. This had brought the claimant to Washington for relief. For twenty years he had had the favorable reports of the legal committees of both branches of Congress. Whenever there was a fair examination of his claims, he always obtained a favorable decision. Yet, some perverse fate had always intervened, and he had just missed the final victory by some absurd or cruel accident.

In recounting the story of this case to my friend, I said to him : " The celebrated Sam Ward once said that one of the great advantages about a despotism was the fact that you either got justice, or you didn't, at once. Here, in our lovely republic, where all men are free and equal in theory, the road to justice for a private individual, in his dealing with the Government of the United States, is a very sharp and stony one. If any individual were to follow the same rule of conduct in the management of his private affairs, as is pursued by the Government of the United States, he would be barred out of decent society. An honest man is supposed to be always anxious to pay his debts, and to place no obstacles in the way of the people who seek to claim money from him upon obligations incurred. Yet, the Government of the United States treats every person who makes a claim against it for money, no matter what the service rendered, as if he were a thief. Each claimant is supposed to be dishonest. It is the unwritten law of every department that no information of any kind shall be given out which may form the basis of a claim against the Government. Suppose the Chief of Bureau knows, from the records in his own office, that the Government owes A a thousand dollars, and A calls to have his account settled. A must prove his case, before the Chief of the Bureau will even give him a footing for his claim ; and if he has to depend upon the Government for his evidence, he can collect nothing, and the Government is placed in the attitude of a deliberate swindler of an honest man. This precaution is taken— that is, the precaution of withholding evidence—to prevent the building up of claims against the Government ; but I claim that the conduct of a government should always be on a par with the conduct of a high-minded and honorable man, and that there should be established, at Washington, a tribunal for the trial of claims against the Government, and that the elements of justice and right alone should be the considerations in their settlement."

I might have gone on further with this subject, for it was one in which I was deeply interested ; but my attention was distracted by the fact that Captain Harcourt, while continually nodding approval, did not look me in the face as he talked, but appeared to be looking intently at something just beyond me. His look of interest was so intense that it gave me a peculiar feeling. There was nothing even suggestive of the uncanny about the Captain ; but it was very clear that he saw something that I could not see, and that he was, in reality, looking at some picture which pleased him very much.

I have never been very backward about asking questions. It has been my trade for some years, and I felt that I knew the Captain well enough now to venture across the line of mere acquaintance and seek to penetrate the peculiarities of his character and disposition. I said, with mock earnestness : " Oh, perfectly happy man, what is it that you see that others do not? It is not the first time I have seen that expression of contentment and enjoyment upon your face at some apparent picture spread before you. Is that the explanation of your tranquility and your contentment? Do you possess means of entertainment and interest beyond those the powers give to ordinary man?"

At first he made no answer, but shifted his attention to my right, and looked as intently beyond me as he had before. There was no appearance of discourtesy upon his part. He simply seemed to be addressing himself to some one just beyond me. I waited a moment, and then he made, slowly, this answer: "I am glad to see that you are to be accorded the privilege which I have so long enjoyed."

"You have so long enjoyed?"

"Yes; ever since I recovered my health on the Island of Nolos. It was there I learned all that has given me my health and my serenity. I came to Washington with a purpose, and that was to leave some one here who should enjoy, upon my departure, all of the faculties of nature which have been developed in me. I shall go to London and to Paris for the purpose of leaving there, let us say, diplomatic representatives of the Island of Nolos. You shall be our ambassador here. You shall have full powers; and it is certain that you will not exchange this ambassadorship for that of the proudest and most powerful nation of the earth."

"The ambassadorship of Nolos! And what, may I ask, are the wonderful powers and privileges of such an ambassadorship?"

The Captain now looked at me directly, as he said : " The representative of the Island of Nolos has the double power of seeing things exactly as they are in contrast with what they should be."

CHAPTER IV.

THE CAPTAIN ASKS ME TO INTRODUCE HIM TO WASHINGTON SOCIETY, AND PROMISES IN RETURN TO INTRODUCE ME TO MY IMMORTAL SOUL.

This brief explanation of the Captain's really explained nothing. I had no opportunity to obtain any more information from him at that particular time, as I was summoned away by an imperative message from the office below. A friend of a life-time was there, on his way to a train, and he had some message, which he thought of great importance, to deliver, so I left the Captain before I had a final understanding. There are many people who think they see things as they are, and so his claim in this regard meant nothing to me. I believe that this is one of the first principles of journalism. I recall, now, a cynical managing editor, who coached me in my earlier days, and who said to me, upon one memorable occasion: "Try and see things as they are; but try and see them awfully lively. Do not be too damnably literal, and use your imagination when the law does not forbid." Captain Harcourt might see things as they really were, and not find that a special object of contentment. Then, too, the contrasting picture of things as they should be, might become a subject for despair, instead of happiness.

After I had finished with the visit of my friend, I received a note from Captain Harcourt, asking me to return to his room that evening. The rest of the day I was occupied with ordinary matters. After dinner, instead of going to my accustomed seat before the fire in the office, I walked up to Captain Harcourt's room, where I knocked, and was told to enter. Here, too, was another open fire, and at one corner sat the Captain, buried in an easy chair. He invited me, by a gesture, to take a seat opposite.

He began his conversation with a question : " Where are you going this evening ? "

" I have no very important engagement—nothing that I would not gladly surrender for the pleasure of a quiet talk with you by this fireside."

" Oh, I don't wish to interfere with any engagement you have. Tell me, where had you intended to go ? "

"There is a reception at the Russian Legation this evening. I had thought of going there, but not before eleven o'clock. There is a little supper at Senator Stanley's, where I may drop in between twelve and one. He is a very intimate friend of mine, and he has insisted upon my coming to him for a little while. Mrs. Captain Spencer has a reception on Massachusetts Avenue, where a lot of nice Army and Navy people are sure to be. I had thought of looking in there, on my way to the legation. Why do you ask? Would you like to go along?"

" Very much."

" I will just step to the telephone, then, and call up the Secretary of the Russian Legation, who is a friend of mine, and ask his permission to bring you with me. I will not have time to send down to Mrs. Spencer; but she is a very good friend of mine, and you, as an old naval officer, will be very welcome.

"But it is rather odd, my dear Captain, that you should want to go at all. I never heard of your going out since you have been here. Each night, I have found you always in the same seat, and in the same attitude, and so supremely contented, that I cannot imagine you now going out from yourself, seeking diversion. Is it possible that the perfectly happy man, who sees things as they are, as well as things as they should be, feels, at last, the desire for a change?"

"It is not exactly that. I am not confined by any law of the Island of Nolos to remain stationary at any particular time, or to confine myself to any prescribed round: I love variety, as you do; but in that variety which, to you, long ago begun to stale, I find that infinite, ever-reaching one which is never wearisome."

It was now nine o'clock; so I observed to the Captain that good things never lose by the waiting. If we were to go out, it was time to dress. And so I said to him: "Did you ask me to come here this evening for no other purpose than to beg of me the privilege of going out with me into Washington society?"

"There was another reason," said he. "I wished to begin to-night the development of your sixth sense."

"But I have arrived at that already. I am a newspaper correspondent," was my reply. "All good newspaper correspondents have, at least, the six senses, and

I have known one or two who thought they had the seventh."

The Captain looked at me gravely. " I'm in earnest," said I. " The gathering of news; the sifting of opinions; the studying of people, occasioned by the duties of a working journalist, do develop in him an odd, intuitive sense, which often, without apparent rhyme or reason, leads him to a result he could not have obtained with the five senses."

Captain Harcourt said: " I can tell you all there is to tell you at present in an hour. Surely, we have time enough for that. You remember that, in my first account that I gave you of the Island of Nolos, I mentioned the name of the doctor who restored me to health. In so doing, he performed a scientific miracle. The doctor was a great Oriental scholar. He was, for many years, an out-and-out Theosophist, and passionately devoted to the study of occult subjects. Soon, even Theosophy became to him tame, and, at the time I knew him, he claimed to have penetrated further into the heart of nature, and in the discovery of its unknown laws, than any mere student of Theosophical Science. He had ransacked the world for information. He spent several years with Keeley in Philadelphia, and he came away from that man enchanted with the discoveries made at the Keeley laboratory. You, yourself, have witnessed some of the tests made by this great man. I call him a great man advisedly. He is the great pioneer discoverer of his age. It is he who has traced out the law of that unknown power, which, opposed constantly to the law of gravitation, is the sustaining element which carries the stars on their swift-flying way through the subtle ether of the universe."

"Yes; I have witnessed some of the tests of Mr. Keeley. I remember, distinctly, the time when he was called a humbug. I suppose that is the fate of every man who is too far ahead of his fellows. I shall never forget the tests made with him, when Professor Raymond went to his laboratory. I was one of the witnesses of that most remarkable display of power, developed by what the world called the Keeley motor. It was an odd idea to see a great engine started by the vibration of chords of music. When the committee, moved to a perfect passion of rage at the possibility of any deception, through their eagerness to examine the engine in question, deranged its cunningly-devised machinery, in a second, a shock passed through its magnificent mechanism, with the resistless force of an earthquake, and a powerful steel shaft was twisted before the face and eyes of the committeemen, as though it had been made of paper. I shall never forget Keeley's despair, and his emotion, at the ruin of his splendid machine, which had cost him so much money."

Captain Harcourt replied to this: "I am glad that you have seen the man and have some appreciation of the importance of his work. Surely, is there not a great unknown power, such as he describes, in the world? What is the power that sustains the stars? What is the subtle element which supplies the electric current? If we had, once, control of that power, then a new era would dawn upon the world. The clumsy devices now employed for heat, motive power, and, even, lighting, would all be changed. There is an inexhaustible force to be had, for nothing, to those who are wise enough to know how to reach it. The time will come when the atmosphere will be illuminated by it. By one phase of this development of power, and through it, the laws of gravitation can be overcome, to the extent that flying machines will become possible.

He then continued: "But this is, apparently, far away from the Island of Nolos and my doctor friend."

CHAPTER V.

THE ISLAND OF NOLOS, WHERE CAPTAIN HARCOURT MET HIS SOUL.

"For the moment, I will not go into any elaborate explanation of my life on the Island of Nolos, nor of the wonderful power of Doctor Longman. He first studied the lore of Occultism in the far East, and, underlying it all, he found a thread that contained a clue to an advance upon the art, as it had been known and practised by the most skillful of the experts. To rise to the powers of an adept, in the ancient school of Occult Science, the student was required to subordinate his physical self for years. He was required to stamp out his passions, and subordinate every element in his nature that had previously given him pleasure. He was required to renounce all human ties, and to banish from his mental dictionary the word woman. Everything in his mind was to be cleansed to the highest degree of perfection. In spite of years of patience and self-denial, at the closing chapter of some final advancement, an impure thought or chance suggestion of ambition, forcing itself into the mind of the aspirant, would secure his absolute rejection. His candidacy was never assured, and, oftentimes, the most faithful work only resulted in final failure. Naturally, the adepts were few in number : as few in

the world are strong enough in character or mind to
arrive at the high plane of self-denial required ; while,
as the difficulties become known, fewer still would desire to become candidates.   It is more in accordance
with the nature of the average mortal to seize the
pleasures near at hand at moderate cost, than to pay a
great price for distant joys.   But, my friend, Doctor
Longman, penetrated far enough into the study of the
high principles of Theosophy to be admitted, finally, as
an adept.   His practical nature has placed him in the
front rank of discoverers, and he has much simplified
this Occult Science, by becoming the pioneer in a new
development.

"It is a well-established fact, that in all the great
developments of nature changes are made slowly.
No great invention is swiftly developed.   Thousands
of minds are often at work upon the same problem :
first, one inventor obtains a clue, and meets with the
usual opposition from the stupid ; then, another clue is
found by some one else ; and, then, perchance, at the
last, there appears a receptive mind that gathers up all
the work of the others, and it receives the final impulse in such a way as to crown the experiment with
success.   The last man is the one who becomes
famous, although he has been only an instrument, like
the rest, to receive some of the impressions which are
constantly being given to the world in the interests of
an advancing civilization.

"As I observed before, the doctor was directed to
go to Philadelphia, after he had finished his Eastern
studies ; and it was with Mr. Keeley that he made the

discovery, which will, in my humble judgment, do so much to revolutionize modern life, and move us up nearer to the ideal existence of happiness, to which every one born in the world is honestly entitled."

" May I ask what that discovery was?"

" Yes; it was the ready and simple means required to introduce each individual to his immortal soul. Everything is simple after that."

" Introduce one to his own soul! You mean in a figurative sense?"

" No ; I mean exactly what I say. He found the means to perform the actual introduction of the individual to his soul, so that he could actually see his soul, and carry on as distinct conversations with the same as can two individuals."

I glanced at Captain Harcourt, as he looked curiously beyond me, from time to time. He was as quiet and serene as ever. I, who had been a professed Materialist all my life, had, at bottom, a rare liking for the mystical, when there was no evidence of vulgar chicanery; and so I turned with pleasure towards the Captain, as I said :

" It must be a delightfully odd and original experience to be able to meet one's own soul. I wonder what kind of soul has long inhabited my poor body. I have wondered if there was any such thing?"

" Any such being, you should say."

"Custom has taught me to speak of the soul as impersonal."

" I know there is no harm in that. Such phrases have been employed because no one, not even the highest adepts, have understood, until recently, the real character of the soul, and the relations existing between the soul and the human habitation it is called upon, from time to time, to occupy. To fully understand this, you must meet your own soul and talk with him. He will have no secrets from you."

"But how can one meet his soul?"

"I will soon make that plain to you, as it was made clear to me by my friend, Doctor Longman. He had been, for years, upon the track of his discovery, when he and I met on shipboard, at the time I was on my way to South Africa to die. The doctor was just returning from Philadelphia, where he had spent three years with Keeley, the greatest inventor of his time. Keeley confines his discoveries to the material world. It is he who, before he dies, will be able to utilize the power that sustains the planets and stars in the Universe, as opposed to the law of gravitation or attraction, which prescribes their orbits. This mighty force is, to-day, registered in the medium of electricity, and made to perform only a tithe of the work it will perform when fully developed. We are very near the time when it will be the motive power of the world, and the source of artificial heat and light, at a cost so slight that climates can be practically changed, and the most sterile soils reclaimed, through the power of this fructifying heat principle."

The Captain, here, continued : "I do not mean, now, to go into the material side of the Keeley motor discovery, but will only allude to the discovery of Doctor Longman, made in the Island of Nolos, after his return with me there. He became attached to me, first, by kindly liking, and then, later, he desired to use me for the purpose of making an experiment. He said to me, then, that I had been given up by all of my physicians, and that I could well afford to try experiments, particularly when they were of a nature that could by no possible means injure me. At this time, I was strangely indifferent to life. It is a compensation, sometimes given one, stricken by mortal disease, by kindly nature. When we arrived at the island, I found the most favorable climate and surroundings.

"The doctor's house, a strongly-built, wide-verandahed cottage, occupied an isolated position upon a bluff, that overlooked the blue sea that surrounded the tiny island. No servants lived in the cottage. The few that were required, occupied quarters on the neighboring grounds. No more beautiful place in the world could have been found for a student. The climate, ever genial and bright; the gentle, serene, luxuriant landscape of wild and cultivated foliage against a background of blue sea, rarely flecked with white, made a surrounding so full of repose, that, here, enchanting dreams come and hardly rival the reality of this poetic and serene isle of the southern seas.

"It was here that the ravages of consumption, that had been devouring me with such rapidity, were checked, and at last were driven out by the powerful aid of my soul."

"Your soul?"

"If it had not been for my soul, and his consent, I would not now be here."

" Do you draw a distinction between the individual I and the soul ? "

" You shall judge yourself. My answer would be, as we now stand, yes and no ; but, pardon me, if I get on as rapidly as possible with my explanation, before I begin to weary you."

" You need not fear that."

" Doctor Longman was greatly aided in his discoveries by his constant communications from the adepts in Thibet, with whom he had so long studied. It was his election to complete his work in the world, although the Island of Nolos, where he spent the greater part of his time, was as much out of the real world as if he were in the mountain fastnesses of Thibet."

" Did he use the regular means of communication, or was he enabled to receive letters sent through space, as I have seen in works descriptive of theosophical wonderment ? "

" No ; all such descriptions are untrue, so far as I understand. The messages were sent to the doctor through means of thought-transference, and were, sometimes, seen in the crystal, as the doctor was a gifted seer of the dark mirror, and could often view events, taking place at the greatest distance, simply with the aid of his Egyptian mirror. But, some day, you will go to the Island of Nolos with me, and then you will learn all about it."

" I go to the Island of Nolos ? "

" Yes ; most assuredly. It is there you will alone become intimate with your own soul. You will receive an invitation from the doctor before my departure from Washington. But, to my own case. Doctor Longman had become convinced, after his studies in Philadelphia, that the essence of the principle sought to be controlled by Keeley for material purposes was, undoubtedly, the life principle which animated man. No one had understood this life principle. It had always escaped analysis. No scientist could locate it, or define it. He could analyze the substances of all materials, and give names to them all; but no power of man could go beyond the material barrier. Man, with all his skill, could not produce even the shadow of the life principle. No savant has ever been able, or will be able, to make the smallest blade of grass. It is the life principle, lying under all creation, that has escaped us all. In the body of man there is a mysterious force, sympathetic and responsive, that escapes diagnosis or analysis. What is it that sends the flash of sensation from nerve to brain, and there records it? What power is it that enables the will to close the hand, to move the legs of the body? What power is it that sustains the involuntary action of the great organs? What mysterious influence is it that checks the action of these organs under the shock of bad news, so that death sometimes intervenes? What is it that often brings a patient back from the gates of death, when physicians and medicines have failed? Let a wave of happiness come, and the life principle, restored by some mysterious influence, sends the dying patient back to health and happiness. What is the will? What makes some men strong and resolute, and others feeble and cowardly? These questions, studied profoundly by Doctor Longman, brought home to him the conviction that the life principle was an emanation of the mighty power, miscalled electricity, and which permeates the imponderable ether of the Universe. The soul, according to his idea, was the directing element of the power ; in other words, the engineer of this mysterious force. The soul is proved to exist in the preliminary study of the adepts; but it was left to Doctor Longman to demonstrate the great possibilities to be found in the study and intimate acquaintance of this subject.

" His first discovery was based upon observance of undisputed fact—that, in illness, whatever contributes to the perfect contentment of the mind of the patient contributes more to his recovery than any medicine. He argued from that, perfect happiness meant perfect health, and he insisted that this world could be advanced when the individual could be made to reach upwards to his proper heritage of perfect happiness. In his studies in Thibet he had learned that much of the unhappiness of the body—that is, disease—was owing to the lack of harmony between the body and the soul occupying it. The soul becomes impatient after a time, when the body is weak and wasted, and is eager to leave it. The withdrawal of its support weakens, instantly, the life principle, and physical collapse follows. Now, his hope with me was in having me with him, under the most favorable conditions. ' In the first place,' said he, ' I shall steep you in happiness. A soul is, naturally, at home only in a perfectly happy body. If I can restore the lost harmony between your soul and your enfeebled body, you will experience possibly the recuperative powers of the life principle, summoned back by the imperious command of the soul.'

"This was the theory of his cure. Through his power he reduced me to a negative condition, and, through the power of his mirror, he introduced me to a sight of the wondrous visions of what was being done throughout the world of spiritual development. By his skill the doctor placed me in such harmonious relations with the divine order of the Universe, that I heard its mystic music for the first time. My heart overflowed with happiness. I saw a world really united, and working for the advancement of all. Such visions as were given me filled me with such an endless source of enjoyment that I forgot all else. But the doctor noted, calmly, that the body was recovering its lost tone; the hidden weakness disappeared. In three months' time, I, my body, was restored to the absolute perfection of health. The doctor was made so happy by this discovery, that he went even further in his demonstrations of the influence of the soul. I will abridge the history of his long experiments, by saying that he finally arrived at the point where he could, without breaking the tie between soul and body, yet so separate them, that the two, as separate intelligences, could see and converse with each other."

" To what end?'

" To the advancement of their mutual interests."

" Mutual interests?"

"Yes; the soul is only finally released from the

lower sphere of existence, when it has occupied the
body of one who has fulfilled all the higher laws, and
has arrived at perfect happiness."

"How did you learn this?"

"In talking with my soul."

"Do you see him often?"

"Every day. He is always with me, and always
visible."

"Are you in constant communication with him?"

"Yes. But I consult him as a friend and an equal.
He is superior to me, as perfection is to imperfection;
but between us there is the most perfect equality of
attitude, and if I were to go contrary to his advice or
suggestion, he would not be angry. His patience is
as infinite as the power from which he emanated."

"Where did you first actually see your soul?"

"It was in the Island of Nolos. It was the last
triumph of the doctor's experiment. My sixth sense
became so highly developed that I was able to see, at
first dimly, my soul, when separated lightly from me
by the doctor. At first, he appeared as a faintly outlined vision. Then his outlines became more positive,
and now, to-day, his proportions and form, are to me as
positive as yours, as you sit opposite me."

"How does your soul appear to you?"

"As an individual. He is myself, perfected. His
appearance is that of my physical body, without flaw
or defect. His body is the perfection of mine. As I
study him, I see wherein I am lacking. My intelligence, my brain, is dominated by a spirit, in contradis-
tinction from the soul. The individual I is here. It

partakes of the imperfections of the body, and only becomes absorbed in the soul, the higher portion, when
the body and spirit are perfected. Here, the organ of
free will permits the spirit to drag the body down.
The spirit and the soul are the real sub-conscious existences in our bodies. There are, apparently, three
lives in one ; but the life of the body, while distinct in
reality, partakes so of the nature of the spirit and the
soul as to be properly subordinated to them. Remember, the soul is perfect and can never be degraded. The
body is under the domination of the spirit. If the
bodily aspirations are high, and sustained by a close relation with the soul, then the spirit becomes free and
soars upward to the higher standard of the soul, with
whom it finally becomes united.

"The action of the spirit is also influenced by other
influences beyond those of its bodily association. When
released by death from an imperfect or low existence,
it associates with rejected spirits of a like class. They
are still united to the higher essence of the soul, which
drives them back to a further existence in the world,
until they can earn the right to a release. The influence
of the spirits of the good, although not yet perfect, hovers
about the existence of those who are given to high aspirations, so that one is more and more impressed with
the strong, upward influence of refined and elevating as-
sociations. This atmosphere of good, or of evil, so clear
to every observer, is created by the influence of the
spirits, who hover around what is most natural to them,
seeking a return to existence in the world, where all are
obliged to work out the primary stages of development."

"Then we have lived many lives? According to your view, the spirit passes through many existences. Supposing this to be true, where can be the advantage, if we have no memory of our past existences. How can we profit by the lessons of the past?"

"The record of these existences is known to the spirit. The individual I, the essence of the life of all, could learn also what he has known in the past, through study of his soul, who knows everything. When one earns the right by perfect living here, then he is promoted to a higher and happier planet, where is made to him a present of a faithful memory of his past, which he can evoke at his pleasure, for the purpose of contrast. The time is now reached, for a few, to make known some of the possibilities of modern psychical developments. It is through acquaintance with my soul that I have learned the way of perfect happiness. But it is only by constant communication with him that I learn all of the laws of such living. With his aid, I see myself as I am, and, through my spiritual visitor, I see him the perfection of myself, what I should be."

"But I should think, as I said before, that this should be for you the source of anything but happiness. To compare your own imperfections with a living standard of perfection, would, I should think, cause you despair?"

"If he were separate, absolutely, from me, this would perhaps be true. But I remember that he is always part of me, and so my constant sight of him is an encouragement. It is the sight of this splendid goal that gives me contentment to walk in any path of en-

deavor, and which will entitle me, some day, to become
united with the perfect self. Then the individual I,
the individuality, whose home is in my mind, united
with my spirit purified, will become blended with my
soul, and be privileged to return to life and communion
in the central abode of happiness and rest."

"Where is that?"

"Of that I know nothing. I know that countless
ages may pass before the final union may be made.
In these long periods of life, and change from the life
of one planet to another, time counts but little.
In the development of the individual, as in the building
of the worlds of space, the element of time is not
to be considered. I do not seek to pierce the future.
I try to live the life that is most pleasing to my soul,
and, in so doing, I have thus far found a happiness,
which has fortified my body against fatigue or disease.
What I now enjoy is the heritage of everyone. If the
vision of the sixth sense were, to-day, to be given to
every one, few would avail themselves of its privileges.
You shake your head. Well, tell me how many there
are, whom you know, who really desire to be better?
You must not only have this desire, but it must become
the ruling impulse of your life, before you can be introduced to your immortal soul."

The Captain continued : "When are we to arrive at
the physical ideal, where one will be made master of
the full powers and capacities nature has placed within
the reach of us all? Who will come and teach us to
live so as to avoid the blunders and crudities of ordinary existence? Who will come and, with the dexterous

art of true knowledge, remove the expression of dis-
content and dissatisfaction from the faces of the mass
of people who have reached middle life?

"Who knows, to-day, a contented and peaceful old
age, dignified, admirable, lovable, that is not so exceptional as to merit the writing of a book to describe its
remarkable character? Look at the faces and forms of
the people who are growing old. Some are lean,
shriveled, with faces lined with envious thoughts;
while others are burly, unshapely, with laxity and self-
gratification puffing every feature of their unwholesome-
looking faces. The mean and the ordinary, in their
onward march to the grave, step in close and serried
ranks, overshadowing, in point of numbers, the select
few who have better learned the lesson of life, and
who have gained some profit where so many find only
the ashes of disappointment.

"Who stands as he should ; who does not walk with a
slouch ; who observes the laws of neatness or of health ;
who dresses with any real care ; who wishes really for
any improvement ; who wants to do what he should, and
who does not contemplate, with pleasure, the thought
of what is conventionally forbidden?"

The Captain looked kindly at me, as he said : "I am
convinced that your dissatisfaction with life, as it now
runs, is as much a sign of a great mental ill health, as
the ill health that troubled me physically when I first
went to the Island of Nolos. Now, I have told you
what I have, to prepare you, yourself, for an introduction to your own soul; for, I am sure that you are to do
good in the world, and that half of your present un-

happiness lies in the fact that you feel yourself in a groove of life, from which there is no outlook that satisfies your real ambition. If you were anxious for the gratification of an ambition, as it is ordinarily understood, I should not have suggested to you what I now shall propose. As soon as you are sufficiently familiar with my plans, and feel in harmony with the same, I shall do for you the kindness performed for me by Doctor Longman, and introduce you to your own soul. I wished to tell you this before going out with you, as you could thus understand better what would have appeared to you as more and more mysterious as our intimacy increased."

"Is your sensitized vision confined to seeing your own soul?"

"Through him, but through him only, can I see the souls of others. It is as he wills. From him I often learn of the condition of men and things that otherwise might have deceived me."

"The secrets of others should be laid bare to you. You are a man to be dreaded."

"On the contrary; the immortal souls are very loyal and never impart any information concerning the individuals to which they are allied, save and except where such information is necessary for the inquirer's well being, or to prevent the one informed against from doing some evil act."

At this I arose. It was now ten o'clock. "Come," said I, "it will take me ten minutes to dress. We will leave here at half-past ten. You have a perfect genius for fairy tales, Captain Harcourt, and I am indebted to

you for a very charming entertainment. Your air of
absolute candor, and tone of deep conviction, made me,
for a time, believe all you have said, in spite of myself ;
but, before accepting one shred of your beautiful and
impossible theory, my dear Captain, I shall have to
wait until——"

"Until when?" he gravely asked.

"Until you actually present me to my own immortal
soul."

"I am quite content to wait until then," said the
Captain, with a smile, as I backed out of his room to
run away to dress.

CHAPTER VI.

THE RECEPTION AT THE RUSSIAN LEGATION.

In a moment more, we entered our carriage, and were driven over the smooth asphalt of the wide streets until the Legation, a massive, square building, half a mile distant to the northwest, was reached. We found this building ablaze with light. Outside, carriages were packed in serried ranks, presided over by mounted police, who kept everything moving, and who hoarsely called out the names of the departing guests, and sped on the vehicles of the arrivals. The sonorous calls of the police under the huge *porte cochère*, where also stood two stalwart Russian *chasseurs*, in full winter livery, buried in furs, were taken up by the drivers down the long line of carriages. The coachmen were nearly all negroes, with powerful high-pitched voices. They chanted the calls with the rich, sweet notes of plantation singers. The negroes enjoyed the excitement and the uproar of the confused circle that surrounded the great lighted house, which stood out in warm relief against the cold driving night. When a departing guest was the happy owner of a title, this was the signal for the negroes on the boxes of the carriages to give unusual emphasis and prolonged notes to their cries. A general of the army, or a senator of the United States, had his carriage called in rapturous notes, which would have done honor to a hosanna to a king. In spite, however, of the seeming confusion, there was underneath a brisk business system, borne of many similar scenes, and which, by its thoroughness, avoided any vexatious delays.

It was after eleven, when we entered the great drawing-room, now packed with a brilliant gathering of the representative people of the best classes of the American Republic. The occasion was an extra-official one, in honor of the Czar's birthday. The diplomats were, therefore, in full court dress, and even the President and his Cabinet were present, gathered in a compact group at the upper end of the drawing-room, where the Russian Minister, a grave, pale-faced bachelor, assisted by the Parisian wife of his First Secretary of Legation, a dark, slim brunette, in white silk and pearls, stood, receiving the guests. The entire Senate of the United States, the eager foreign types of the diplomatic colony, the principal members of the House, the army and navy officers, in full uniform, with the ladies of high official society, made a gathering interesting and picturesque from point of color, character, and good taste. Nearly every man present was notable, and had his name written in large capitals in the book of the nation. The babel of tongues, which rose and fell like the waves of the sea, included nearly every modern language. The vivacity and formality of manner of the foreigners was in striking contrast with the self-contained, easy dignity of the American types. There was nowhere visible any attempt at self-assertion. Nearly every one present was a distinct somebody, conscious of his footing in the world, and, therefore, careless whether such fact was overtly recognized or not. Among the public men one could hardly find a so-called swell; yet, all were correctly dressed, although an occasional carelessness in some point of detail, never overlooked by one who gives his mind to dress, alone, rather marked the superiority of the type. These public men, many of whom had passed the greater part of their lives in some small provincial town, basked at their ease in the full glare of the brilliant gathering, and studied the faces of those with whom they came in contact with the calmness of men very sure of themselves. Trained to appear before the public, and to bear with the front of stoics the fiery ardors of combative debates, these same men found themselves so at home in a crowd, that even the political novices to Washington society appeared like veterans. The complimentary effusiveness of the Southern men, and the animation of the Southern women, gave a touch of color to the graver manners of the Western and Eastern types. The Western and the Southern guests appeared most in sympathy with each other; but, throughout the whole assemblage, there was the familiar touch of good fellowship found in a harmonious family. The compliments, the gay speeches, and the scandal talked at any such reception, would fill volumes. It is in such gatherings that news of coming events is gathered with the greatest skill by the gossip-lovers. Every true member of Washington society loves gossip, and the statesman who would keep his plans to himself would do well to keep out of the Washington houses, where, under the stimulus of friendly meeting, even the most rigid and reserved unbend, and babble and chatter, like so many school-children. The ladies in such a society carry everything before them, and some of the best-kept secrets escape in such an atmosphere of gayety, and fly about from under one fan to another, until the swiftness of the telegraph is quite eclipsed, and the most energetic news-gathering systems of modern newspapers are put quite to shame.

As we paused for a moment before the Russian Minister, he gave us a smiling, civil word, and then passed us on to Madame Neville, who stood on his right. There was a pause in the movement of the guests as we came up, and, for a moment, no one came to say farewell.

Madame Neville looked straight at Captain Harcourt, as she said : " I have never had the pleasure of seeing you before. Are you a late arrival in Washington ? "

" No, madame. As a former officer of the navy, I once lived here a long time. I have returned for a winter, and this is my first public appearance."

" I have heard of you before, Captain Harcourt."

" Indeed."

" Yes ; I recently had a letter from Paris concerning you. You remember Captain Maxime de Berthier ? "

" Very well, indeed. We are intimate friends."

" He has written me such a pretty tale concerning your home in the Island of Nolos, and even more."

" And more ? "

"Yes; more. He says that you are a man who has probed all mysteries, and even the greatest mystery of all."

The Captain bowed, without a word.

Madame Neville said, now, with a bow of dismissal, turning in the direction of some approaching guests: "I hope to see more of you, Captain Harcourt. Monsieur de Berthier is a *cousin german*, and he has written so much about you, my desire to see you and talk to you has grown with his description. I am at home on Tuesdays to my special friends."

Captain Harcourt saluted profoundly, and we moved on.

A word or two of this conversation was heard, and then passed on. In a few moments these words were exaggerated, so that my companion received as much attention as was paid to the President of the United States, who, protected by the body-guard of his Cabinet officers and higher officials, was the constant subject of scrutiny of the curious, polite, good-natured throng, which sought, by studying his impassive face, to gather the denial or affirmation of some one of the numerous reports flying about concerning him, or his action relating to this or that private or public affair. It was upon such occasions as these, that the ever-present, never-dying, intimate friend of the President, whose name is never known, is so frequently quoted concerning the private thoughts of the chief magistrate, who holds in his mighty hands the dispensing of favors, upon which depend the ambition and political prosperity of the greater number present.

We were accosted, at every turn, by an acquaintance or a friend. All sought introductions to Captain Harcourt. There appeared to be a nameless attraction about him. An adroit question, here and there, by some active-minded lady, brought out the residence of Captain Harcourt. Then this passed rapidly around, until Captain Harcourt, the mysterious representative of the Island of Nolos, took his unquestioned position as the latest, and, therefore, the most interesting notability in a society made up of distinguished and noteworthy people.

In one of the sudden movements of the crowd in the direction of the supper room, the Captain and I found ourselves in an alcove, where stood Senator Norton, then one of the most conspicuous and powerful orators and politicians in the upper branch of Congress. He was, at that time, in the prime of a powerful manhood. His pride was as unyielding as his ability was great. He was tall, with the broad shoulders, deep chest and powerful thews of an athlete. He had the pose and gravity of an Indian chief. His head was large, and thickly covered with a silvery mane of hair, that hung in careless profusion around his smooth-shaven, clearly-cut, aquiline features. His complexion was a clear, pale olive. His resolute lips were shaded by a long, drooping mustache. At that time he was the object of great attention, on account of his personal antagonism to the President. Once intimate friends, and still members of the same party, they were now deadly enemies, engaged in a political war as relentless in character as the fiercest of religious conflicts.

The Senator touched me upon the shoulder, as I was passing, and said: "Come to my hotel, when you leave here. I will be able to tell you something to interest you."

"I have a friend with me, Captain Harcourt. Permit me to present him."

"You can bring him along. It will make no difference. The Ambassador of Nolos, who probes all mysteries, may find there a subject worthy, even, of his attention."

Already the Senator had heard of my friend, and made the same allusion to his power that I had heard hinted at every turn a few moments after the conversation with Madame Neville.

The invitation of the Senator gave me a keen sense of surprise. The haughty Senator was little given to taking newspaper correspondents into his councils, and his invitation meant that he had come to some resolution, and was now ready to make public some move in the game he was playing to checkmate the power of his former political chief.

As we turned to leave the house, a moment after the Senator's departure, Captain Harcourt said: "I thought you would need me this evening, and that is the reason I asked you to bring me along with you."

CHAPTER VII.

A REMARKABLE SCENE IN SENATOR NORTON'S PRIVATE DRAWING-ROOM.

It was past midnight, when we entered the long suite of rooms occupied by the Senator. The apartment of six rooms was ablaze with light, and the communicating doors were thrown open. The Senator had a love for splendid theatrical effects, and he nearly always rehearsed every scene in his public career, after the fashion of a great actor. Indeed, I have learned to look upon successful public men as finished actors, possessing qualities which would have won for them success upon the theatrical stage as high as that reached by them in the forum of politics.

Every senator and member has at his disposal the floral treasures of the Government Botanical Garden. The Senator had availed himself of this privilege in the adornment of his drawing-room. Potted plants in the corners made a rich contrast to the blaze of color found in the huge baskets of flowers, scattered about the room in reckless profusion. The room might have been the reception room of a successful *prima donna*, after an evening of triumph, rather than that of a public man, engaged in the grim war of politics.

After all, politics, as played upon national boards, is a stupendous game, in which I have always taken a passionate interest. Politics is the science of human government, and, in its fierce contests, intellectual gladiators are developed, who take rank with the successful heroes of war.

So it was with more than ordinary interest that I entered the Senator's private quarters. It was not the first time that I had been treated to such a careful dramatic presentation as a preliminary to some public demonstration. Senator Norton, like many men of imperious nature in public life, had no use for newspapers, except as mediums to reach swiftly, upon rare occasions, a special public. For all other purposes he would have confined the newspaper press to the barest statements of the facts of current history, condensed to the briefest space, so as to give room for the verbatim reports of the debates of Congress. He was not rich, but he was a lawyer of high rank, and his prominence in the Senate gave him occupation for all of his leisure in the Supreme Court, so that he had a large income, which hardly kept pace with his extravagance. He had always with him a crowd of familiars, who echoed his very sentiments, and gave to him the adulation his nature craved for every waking moment. He had but few friends, in the ordinary sense of the word. His sense of honor was excessive, and his loyalty to those who followed him very great. He divided the world into two classes: those who adhered to him, and those who opposed him. For the former, he was always willing to work; for the latter, he was untiring in his ferocious energy to destroy. It was not enough for him to defeat an enemy. It was neces-

sary for his complete satisfaction to absolutely annihilate him.

So, with a fighter of this character, then engaged in a
personal war with the President, any move upon his
part was certain to make a great sensation with the
public.

We were invited to take seats in great leathern
chairs, placed near the center of the room. The colored servant, who had ushered us in, promptly retired,
shaking with fear, anxious to escape the atmosphere of
tragedy, made evident by the Senator's solemn manner.

The Senator was very much excited, although under
his usual self-control.

He paced up and down throughout the room, beginning to speak in a low tone, which, gradually, increased in volume, until his voice resounded throughout
the drawing-room, as if he were delivering an oration in
the Senate chamber. Indeed, this notable Senator very
often combined as much stage effect, as complete a
dramatic pose, and as much oratory upon a private
audience as upon a public one. He was always at his
best in a personal controversy; when rehearsing a
personal grievance, his vocabulary was wide, ornate
and varied in its tremendous reach of differing
phrases of sneering savagery and contempt. As he
marched up and down, he did not make, at first, any
direct explanation of his invitation. He seemed to take
it for granted that I understood his ways and methods
well enough, and that, before the visit would be finished,
there could be no possibility of a misconstruction of
what he wished to be done. He began with a formal

parade of the character and history of the great party
to which he belonged. In it had been bred chieftains,
who had fought for principles, and who had, by the development of great powers, won a place of lasting regard with the public. But, as the history of the party
proceeded, the Senator swiftly passed to what he
called its "latter day phases"—the day when principles
were forgotten, and personal ambitions were the only
issues. We were then treated to a chapter of ethics, in
which gratitude was defined as an extinct virtue, and
loyalty and truth eliminated from the game of politics.
He did not remain long in the field of generalities. He
now passed, rapidly, along to a sketch of his past relations with the President of the United States. The
President had formerly been one of his lieutenants.
For a long time he had been only too glad to take
orders from the Senator, who had heaped upon his
head countless favors, in return for services rendered.
By a strange chapter of incidents, which the Senator
was pleased to call the "accidental jugglery of events,"
this "man" had been promoted, with lightning-like
rapidity, from relative obscurity to the highest position
of power in our world of politics. The Senator, now,
walking with a slower stride, and speaking with a graver
accent of satire, said :

"Nature has created but few types capable of bearing with equanimity a too sudden and overwhelming
prosperity. Even the strongest are taxed in their
effort to remain upon the same plane of thought concerning themselves. The dangerous intoxication of
vanity threatens every man who has been moved sud-

denly up to an unexpected position of power. It is so easy for one to believe that he is a man of destiny, and that a fate, gifted with a divine intelligence—and not a cruel and brutal accident—has marked him for such advancement. The 'feather-head' in politics," said the Senator, coining a phrase, "mounts with the ease and lack of thought of the thistle-down, and, at a dazzling height, forgets all past alliances, all previous friendships, all prior obligations of duty and loyalty, and becomes the creature of his own stupendous fancies, and imagines that his personality, which, to him, has now become sacred, can make a law unto itself for every future relation in life. The smaller the man, the more complete the desire to annihilate all memory of the prior causes which elevated him so high. The small man, in high place, can afford to have no friends. He must be free from every human influence. If he should permit himself an alliance with any one about him, if he should allow the influence of some past friend to control him, he would lose in his own estimation. Then those who persist still in believing the mere change of residence from private station to an official one cannot, by such transposition alone, enlarge the faculties of the person so transposed, might venture to suggest that this person, or—if you please—this uplifted potentate, is, after all, an ordinary man, and in the leading strings of men who made him." As the Senator finished this thought, he closed, in a mock, chanting voice, as he said: "Here endeth the first lesson."

This discourse had run on for, at least, two hours.

Its conclusion was sharp, and was the climax of the skillful presentation of the story which the Senator had given me to be used as the basis for an article, which would give, in concrete shape, his first open and direct attack upon the President himself.

With what emotion did I listen to this last and concluding chapter in his discourse! How little the Senator knew of my personal relations. I should have been the last person to be selected as his confidant. The story which he told concerned the honor of one of my personal friends, a member of the Cabinet at that time. He was a manly, upright man, as I knew him, devoted to his work, and possessing a reputation of unimpeachable integrity. In rank, he was nearly the first in the President's Cabinet. He was, himself, a good fighter, and had directed many a skillfully-devised attack upon Senator Norton, and it was with an air of aggressive triumph that the Senator flaunted, over the center-table near me, the documents and pieces of evidence going to show a clear and positive case of bribery of the Cabinet officer in question. Certain official favors in his department had been sold for money, and that money had been traced directly home to him. The Senator proposed to move with great rapidity and decision in exposing the infamous character of the transaction. Himself a man of high honor, he never would have stooped to use a foul weapon in fighting an enemy; but, with legitimate weapons, no one could be more unsparing than he. What he proposed to me, indirectly, through this exposition, was, that I should publish the facts of these charges, to be supported by the evidence, which was to remain in the Senator's hands. Then one of his political lieutenants in the House was to move an inquiry, which would be promptly followed by the presentation of articles of impeachment.

In spite of the evidence, I believed that there was some horrible mistake. I could not believe that my friend could have failed in any essential requisite to an honest man. He had too much intelligence to be involved in such a vulgar intrigue for place. I more than suspected that the guilt, which was so apparent in the documents, would be traced to some one else— however, so near to him as to involve him, in spite of his innocence. I knew his wife to be so ambitious of social position as to be absolutely reckless in reaching for the object of her desires. She was a handsome brunette, of a vigorous, physical type; a woman of eager appetites, and possessing a keen desire to shine and lead. ˙Her husband's modest fortune must have been insufficient to satisfy her requirements, and I had noticed, within the last year, associated with her, from time to time, the oily and diplomatic stars of political intrigue, the aristocratic purveyors of position. Their contiguity and assiduity had led me to think that she was in danger of selling her fair name and the honorable position of her husband in her reckless desire to have money. There is, at the elbow of every person of power in Washington, a kind, adroit, complacent individual, who is only too happy to assist financially those who can, at the proper time, give him in exchange something which influence can readily give; but such creditors are dangerous—for every loan advanced they demand the pound of flesh. And so, in this story, which lay bare before me, I fancied I saw the true sequel of the chapter in official life that I had noted since my return.

I, for one, am no half-way friend. To all practical purposes, my friend is myself. This stab at the reputation of a friend came home to me like a hand at my throat. The Senator was a man who could not be easily deceived. The slightest hesitation on my part would have made me an object of suspicion, and the story which had been offered me would, assuredly, be placed in the hands of some other correspondent, who would have no personal reasons for withholding such a sensation. It might be asked here, if I was truly serving my newspaper in desiring, in my heart of hearts, to suppress such a story as that. The only rule in a case of this kind is a man's own conscience. I have always believed that a correspondent is more honestly serving the true interests of his paper by suppressing personal scandals than by publishing them.

I sought to gain time, by asking the Senator to permit me to investigate the character of the story fully and completely, before taking up the question of publication. This made him impatient; but, with an air of a monarch, who yields, benevolently, a request preferred by a subject, consented to give me forty-eight hours. " In case of your failure, I will have the whole facts recited in a resolution, to be presented in the House, as the basis of a request for an official investigation into the conduct of this man." The Senator instinctively felt that there was a shadow of antagonism in my attitude.

Up to this time, he had paid no attention to Captain Harcourt, who had remained silent and observant, following, with a curious and quiet attention, the involved and spectacular oratorical display of the Senator. Something in his manner roused the latter as a challenge. Turning to him, he said, sarcastically: "What does the Ambassador from the Island of Nolos think of my programme of retaliation?"

It was such a condescension for the Senator to ask any one's opinion concerning any course once determined upon by him, that such a question came to me as a surprise. The diversion gave me an opportunity to collect my wits. The Captain met the Senator's question by saying, very simply and very directly:

"My dear sir, I would not have thought of volunteering my opinion; but you have asked it, and I will give it. I do not approve of your line of action."

There was such a gentleness and such a sincerity in the Captain's attitude, as he said this, that the Senator, morbidly sensitive to anything approaching criticism, was not even offended.

He paused in his walk, and came over and took a seat in front of us. Lighting a huge, black cigar, he said, after the first puff of blue smoke: "I am curious to hear the reasons for your disapproval." The Senator's manner had completely changed. He was now quiet and self-contained. There was an alert look of inquiry, however, in his eyes, which foreshadowed a storm of irritability, should the Captain fail in tact and diplomacy in the wording of his reply.

Captain Harcourt looked, with that unmoved expression of tranquility habitual to his face, at the Senator, as he said : " Pardon me, if I speak plainly. Such a contest is not worthy of your high talents and attainments. Such a weapon is beneath the dignity of your real character."

The Senator's face flushed deeply, and then turned a stony white, as, with great deliberation, he said, with icy politeness :

"I have asked for your opinion, and I thank you for your free expression of it." He then arose, and dismissed us, with almost royal curtness, adding to me, as I turned to go: " I shall expect to see you here to-morrow at twelve o'clock, and your decision concerning the publication must be made within the forty-eight hours."

The gray, icy dawn of a cold, sleety morning whipped us in the face, as we left the Senator's hotel, and walked across the snow-covered square to our own hotel. I was worn with excitement. My friend, the Captain, showed no sign of weariness, and when he bade me good morning, at the door of his room, I heard him give orders for his bath and breakfast, as if he had no idea of going to bed at all.

CHAPTER VIII.

A STUDY OF THE DISTANT ISLAND OF NOLOS, AS VIEWED IN THE DARK SURFACE OF AN EGYPTIAN MIRROR.

After taking a few hours' sleep, I went to Captain Harcourt's room to consult with him—to ask his advice as to the best course to be pursued. I was never more impressed with his ability to see clearly the best thing to be done. I found him waiting for me. He was seated before a table, in the small sitting-room of his private apartment. Upon the table, before him, lay a large, black, Egyptian mirror, set in a heavy silver frame. A dark screen was placed at each side of the mirror, for the purpose of guarding its surface from the rays of any reflected light. As I entered, the Captain signaled to me with his left hand to be seated near him. He was looking, intently, into the mirror, and appeared to be very much occupied.

After several moments of silence, he turned towards me, and said: "Now I am ready for you. I was occupied, for the moment, when you came in, in talking with Doctor Longman."

"In talking with Doctor Longman? I do not understand you."

"You are not familiar, then, with the ancient art of crystal gazing?"

I shook my head.

The Captain said: "By the aid of this dark mirror I am able to see Doctor Longman when I please. At a given hour in the day, he goes to his laboratory and seats himself in front of his mirror. We, both, see each other in these mirrors at the same point of time, and, through a well-established code of signs, can carry on as intimate a conversation as if we were actually together in the same room. You need not look incredulous. This ability to see such visions in a mirror of this kind, or in a clear crystal, is quite common. You may have the ability yourself. Take my place here at the table, and look into this mirror quietly, without excitement, and see if you cannot make out something. Wait a moment; I will tell the doctor to wait for you—that you are going to try and place yourself in communication with him. I know you are in a great hurry to be going upon the business of your friend, the Cabinet officer. But you will find that there is no need of haste, and that you may receive, here, in this room, the assistance necessary to counteract the evil effect of this possible scandal."

I now took the Captain's seat. The perfect simplicity and sincerity of his manner had so impressed me that it seemed the most natural thing in the world to sit down before this mirror and try to find, in its depths, the interior of a laboratory upon the Island of Nolos, on the other side of the world. I looked, tranquilly, upon the black surface of the mirror for several moments, without perceiving anything. I was about to speak, when a gray shadow began to steal across it like a mist. The gray shaded into a steely blue, and then faded again. The shadows now came with great rapidity, with increasing shades of density. Suddenly, out of the mist, there burst a clear, dazzling light, in which danced the colors of a prism. This kaleidoscopic effect endured but a few seconds; then the mirror cleared, and assumed a depth of perspective, which made me lean forward, with great eagerness, close over its surface. I, now, saw distinctly, as through the lens of a powerful telescope, the interior of a room, which, from its furniture and its surroundings, was, clearly, a laboratory.

In the center of this room I saw a distinguished-looking man. He looked directly at me, and he seemed so near that I could not prevent myself from attempting to address him, as if I were, actually, in his presence. The occupant of the laboratory was an old man. His hair was thick and white, falling, in great masses, upon each side of his large, powerful head. His face was broad, pure and clean in its lines. It was devoid of mustache or beard. The features were fine, and regular as those of a cameo. Over all there was an expression of tranquility and power that attracted with the force of a magnet. The high character, the great ability and the gentle spirit were so clearly manifest, as to mark him as an unusual character, although then known only in the distant East as a recluse, who spent the greater part of his time in his laboratory, on the Island of Nolos.

He smiled upon me with such benevolence that I felt, at once, the strongest desire to be placed in communication with him—to exchange more than the greetings of a glance. Here was a higher authority than any I had ever known. It was no wonder, now, to me, that Captain Harcourt had found, in his company and teachings, such wisdom. In his companionship he had acquired the tranquility, and the repose, which had made him so prominent a figure in the restless society of Washington, at the very moment of his appearance in it. Without turning, for fear the vision would fade, I said to Captain Harcourt: "I really do see the laboratory in the Island of Nolos, and Doctor Longman, as you have often described him to me. I wish that I had your knowledge of communicating with him, so that I could ask him a few questions. I never have seen any one who gives me such a feeling of confidence in his wisdom and in his power."

Captain Harcourt, in reply to this, said: "You can be easily taught, and you will be surprised to find how natural and simple it all is. The superiority and the strength of Doctor Longman come from his elevation of spirit. He is more closely allied to his soul than any one I know. He has risen nearer the heights occupied by his soul than any Occultist of modern times. It is through his exalted station, that he now takes in the whole world in his range of vision, and he is now seated, steadily working to do his part in raising up the mass of humanity to the standard occupied by himself and his associates. You will find that the place to begin any work of this kind is in the capital of the country sought to be influenced. In the capitals of the world, politics is the most dominant and power-

ful force. You find yourself, at this particular moment, under the shadow of a violent political intrigue,
the object of which is to gratify a feeling of revenge,
and to produce pain and humiliation to others. The
politics of this country, to-day, is controlled by such
feelings. The high power and influence of leaders is
perverted to gratify selfish and improper ends. Take
the case of Senator Norton, whom we saw last night.
Here is a man with great gifts and the power to impress and to lead others, rarely given to any one individual. The intellectual gifts and the personal charms
of such a man should carry him a great way in influencing the character of a nation. But, to-day, his
entire talent and power are diverted to personal
objects. His entire contention with the President relates to an office. The whole controversy relates to a
favor desired, and a favor refused. American politics,
from the beginning to the end, is, to-day, a chase after
place, and the leaders are those who can capture and
control the most places. The finest abilities and the
highest characters soon become dwarfed in a contest
for such ignoble objects. In the history of this
country, there have been a few great periods. During
the late Civil War, for a time, these personal objects of
petty intrigue were driven aside by the great question
of the salvation of the country itself. In the atmosphere of that time, great sacrifices were made, and
the leaders, then, were conspicuous by their magnificent self-denial. There never was a period of
history in this country when we had greater examples
of the forgetfulness of self. Such an atmosphere

bred great men—men whose names will go down to undying history. Now, I believe that the world can be stimulated to as high deeds, and to as great developments, in times of peace, as was brought forth by the cruel stimulus of a war, or of a revolution."

Captain Harcourt now stood up. Then he changed the subject, abruptly, as he said : " Kindly say farewell, for the moment, to the Island of Nolos." I, involuntarily, bowed to the vision in the mirror, and, to my surprise, the figure responded, with gravity, and with a smile, which seemed to say : " To our better acquaintance." In an instant, the mirror was as black as night, and the vision had disappeared.

I now turned to Captain Harcourt, and said : " I wish to talk with you about a plan of action. I have forty-eight hours to decide about this publication. To a certain extent, the communication made to us by the Senator was a confidential one, although he intends to take public action. Until such action is taken, I am, to a certain extent, bound. I do not feel that I have a right to go to my friend and tell him what is hanging over him. In the first place, if I can avoid this publication, and persuade Senator Norton to take up some other course, I am certain that a serious tragedy will be avoided. My friend is passionate, high-spirited, and if what I see in those papers proves to be true, his family will be broken up, and his public career ended in disgrace. Such a calamity would mean much more to him than death by torture. Now, what would you advise ? "

" You will remember that I once said to you that, in

the Island of Nolos, we were first taught to see things as they are, and then as they should be. We will see how this principle can be applied to this particular intrigue, which is illustrative of the character of this modern development in American politics. Let us see if we cannot save two men from the effects of an infamous act, for it is clearly demonstrable that Senator Norton will be the one upon whom the weight of misfortune will really fall, rather than upon his victim. This is really the law of every unworthy revenge. I have two suggestions to make to you. One is to first go to General Starr, who, you know, is an intimate friend of Senator Norton's and an associate senator. He is also a friend of the President's. I should tell him, frankly, the whole story, and follow his advice. When you return here this evening, we will sit down with our mirror, and we will be able to watch the movements of the leaders in this ignoble fight. That will give you a certain advantage. I cannot now promise that we will succeed absolutely in thwarting Senator Norton in his plans. His imperious nature is subject to but few influences, owing to his hardened armor of self-esteem. It may be that he will be permitted to go ahead and do his worst. The tragedies of life are common."

To this I now said: "If I fail with General Starr, I shall stand upon no small scruples of conscience concerning the seal of confidence indirectly placed upon me by Senator Norton. My friend's life is threatened as seriously as if an assassin had already raised his knife to plunge it in his heart. I will first see General

Starr, and, if necessary, go to the President and to my friend."

With this, I rushed from the room, promising to return in the evening to make a report of the result of my afternoon's work.

CHAPTER IX.

THE FIGHT BETWEEN SENATOR NORTON AND THE PRESIDENT OUTLINED.

As I left Captain Harcourt's rooms and passed through the hotel office below, on my way to keep my appointment with Senator Norton, I met a messenger, who handed me a note, in which I was informed that the Senator would see me late that evening, as he had been obliged to go to the Supreme Court, upon a matter of urgent importance.

This note pleased me. At least, that much time was saved. I now proceeded at once to the Capitol building to find General Starr. I knew I would either find him in his committee-room, or in the Senate chamber, as he never was absent, without serious reasons, from the Capitol after twelve o'clock, the hour of the beginning of the regular sessions. General Starr represented one of the great Western States in the Senate. No member of that powerful body was more respected than he. He had held public posts nearly all his life, by which he could have easily made himself rich; but no dishonest dollar had ever stained his generous hands. His poverty, his honesty, his straightforward ways, and his blunt speech made him one of the most conspicuous men of his time.

He was one of the most daring and reckless of the

soldiers of the Civil War. He rose to high rank, and every step of his advancement was earned by some special deed of valor. He was a natural-born soldier, and, when brought into fierce competition with the trained soldiers of West Point, was ranked as the equal of the best, and came out of the contest one of the volunteer heroes of the time. I found him in his committee-room, seated at the end of a long table, dictating letters to a stenographer. Upon his right and left were masses of private correspondence, the accumulation of numerous petitions for place and official favors. As a former soldier of distinction, he was looked to by the veterans, throughout the country, as their personal agent, to whom they could freely apply for any information concerning their claims for pensions. The amount of business, for which the Senator could receive no pay, would have staggered a first-class lawyer's office in the City of New York. Yet, he went, two hours every day, patiently through drudgery of this kind, before making his appearance in the Senate chamber to attend to his public duties.

He turned, with impatience, at being interrupted in his work, as he said, with his usual curt directness: "You must have something important to talk to me about, to come in upon me at this hour."

"It is a matter of importance," I replied.

"Can't you wait until this evening to tell me about it?"

"If it were a matter personal to myself, I should say yes, at once; but, I think, you should know first the ground facts, which can be quickly told, and then you, yourself, shall decide whether you can afford to give your time to it now."

I asked the Senator to take me into the inner room of his quarters, so that I could talk to him alone. He declined to move from his seat. He said: "You need not mind my private secretary over there. He never hears anything that I don't want him to hear, and if he should, would forget it. We have too many secrets told here, for one, or more, or less, to make any special impression. My secretary was my chief staff-officer during the war, and he is my second self."

Briefly, then, I told what I had heard from Senator Norton, the night before. The General puffed, leisurely, at a black cigar while I talked. He made no comment, and betrayed not the slightest shadow of excitement. When I had finished, he said: "It is an affair that can wait. If you like, come and see me this evening, at my house."

I was stung by his seeming indifference. I knew him to be a devoted and loyal friend. His relations with the threatened Cabinet officer were most intimate, and had endured through a number of years. I could not understand his perfect tranquility, his absence of excitement, and his apparent amusement at my agitation and impatience.

In answer to some of my remarks, expressive of surprise at his attitude, the Senator said: "You correspondents, at best, are mere amateurs in politics. You are only spectators. You never descend to the arena and encounter the blows of an actual contest. You are only too ready to jump to hasty conclusions, and, not having, always, abundant sources of information, although you all think you have, you are too ready to form judgments concerning the motives of others. I am not indifferent to what you have told me; but what is the use of getting excited about it? I have no time to waste on emotions of that kind. Besides, I know Senator Norton better than you do. He is a magnificent artist, in his way, and he only uses extreme measures when necessary to carry his end. He is much better informed than you in everything that relates to life in Washington. It is on account of his knowledge of your relations with that Cabinet officer that he selected you as his confidant. He told you the story, with the certainty that you would carry it straight to the Cabinet officer in person, or, failing that, to the President himself. It is a mere move in a game. He wants to make the President back down and withdraw the man that he has nominated for Collector of the Port in his State. That is all that he wants to accomplish. He may, possibly, add a condition, that one of his own particular men shall be put in his place. Will the President consent? I do not know. He, himself, is a very obstinate man, and as much of an egotist as Norton. Whether your friend, the Cabinet officer, and my friend as well, will get smashed in the affair, will depend upon the kind of management we employ. I should advise the President to yield. Norton has a very strong hand, and he will play it for all it is worth. Although you may be sure that he is more anxious than you to avoid an actual publication."

It was hard for me to emulate the Senator's Oriental tranquility.

"What shall I do, meanwhile, until I see you again?" said I.

The Senator smiled, sarcastically. "If you are very hard up," said he, "for something to do, you might turn in and go to work on some of these letters." He then added, at my look of consternation at this proposition: "Why do you want to make such an infernal busybody of yourself over this matter, anyway? It is a play, in which you can take no conspicuous part, without doing more harm than good. If you really wish to serve your friend, obey my orders, and, for the time being, go on, as if nothing were known to you. You come to see me this evening, at ten o'clock. I then may have something to suggest to you. Above all, keep away from Senator Norton. He is, altogether, too adroit for you, and the less you see of him the better. Let him think what he pleases. He has given you forty-eight hours in which to act, and he knows that, under no circumstances, would you publish those documents. He will wait, with great tranquility, for the counter-move from the President."

"But do you not think our friend, the Secretary, should know?"

The Senator now turned towards his private secretary. "I have given you all the time I intend to, this morning. I have outlined a plan of action for you. Try and follow it. Hold your tongue; and, if you have got anything else in the world to do, aside from this business, attend to it."

I was dismissed in a brusque and friendly fashion. After leaving the Senator's committee-room, I could not refrain from going up into the Reporters' Gallery of the Senate to see if Senator Norton was in his seat. This was not following General Starr's advice strictly ; but I had never served in the army, and construed my orders with the liberality of a man of imagination, stimulated by the highly-developed curiosity of my profession.

Senator Norton, dressed with the care, precision and elegance which marked him one of the great dandies of the Senate, walked down the center aisle of th e cham ber, as I sank into my seat in the gallery. Apparently, he saw no one. He took his seat, and began opening letters, which lay in a small pile in front of him. Some dull, droning debate, upon a subject of a routine character, was going on. The galleries were nearly empty. But few senators were in the chamber. Suddenly, the doors of the great entrance chamber were thrown open, and a slight figure of a man, of medium height, attired in a close-fitting, dark, frock-coat suit appeared in the portals. The venerable captain of the pages, who is the host of the Senate upon the occasion of any official call, darted forward to receive the visitor, who carried, under his right arm, a huge, white, square envelope, sealed with a flare of red wax.

The gavel of the presiding officer descended with a whack, as the visitor and the captain of the pages faced about in military attitudes of attention. The visitor was the private secretary of the President of the

United States. Standing like a man of wood, the private secretary, in a weak, piping voice, said : " Mr. President."

The Chair replied : " Mr. Secretary."

The secretary saluted, and said : " Mr. President, I have the honor to submit to the Senate, from the President of the United States, a message in writing."

The envelope was then handed to the chief page, and carried by him to the presiding officer, the private secretary retiring quickly from the floor. The Chairman of the Senate tore open the envelope, and disclosed a list of official nominations sent in by the President for that day. This bulletin of official favors is one of the events of the day in the Senate. The daily distribution of prizes is always eagerly scanned. Some of the less dignified senators crowded up, with the eagerness of school boys, about the chair to read, over his shoulders, the names of the fortunate selections. Upon this particular occasion, there was a buzz of excitement, and of turning of heads in the direction of Senator Norton, which caused the head of that haughty personage to rise with ready suspicion, foreseeing, instantly, another blow at his power and position from the hands of the President.

It was only too true ; the President had not been content with nominating to the most important office in the Senator's State a person most obnoxious to him, but had followed up this by sending in, upon this particular day, the name of a conspicuously devoted enemy of Senator Norton's for one of the great European missions.

This second affront made a great sensation ; and, in order to measure the full weight of such an attack, one must fully understand the character and nature of the body known as the Senate of the United States, in its actual relations with the President. The Senate is one of the most conservative bodies in the world. The term of office in that body is longer than a Presidential term. A senator who fulfills his duties has a better opportunity for re-election than the incumbent of any other elective office in our country. Many senators, practically, hold life positions, being elected, from time to time, without opposition. The body has the compact and harmonious feeling of a great family. Senators differ among themselves widely, at times; but, upon all questions relating to their privileges, the Senate is a united corporation. It is unswerving in its upholding of the traditions of the past, and in its assertion of its own independence and character. This is as it should be. The Senate is responsible to itself, and, in turn, to the States. It is not responsible to the President, and it possesses a position as unqualifiedly independent as his own ; and has as clear a right to its own opinion as has the President, and is obliged to give him no explanation for any of its acts. Within recent times, numerous contests have grown up between the President and individual senators, growing out of disputes over office. The public has, nearly always, sided with the President : holding that he has the right to nominate whom he pleases, and that it is the Senate's duty to confirm, without opposition, the edicts of the White House. In the original creation of the

power of the President, he was given the great authority of initial action in the selection of the incumbents
of all of the official positions in the country. He has
the power, also, to begin proceedings, as the basis of
the treaty negotiations. He can make suggestions,
from time to time, to Congress, concerning legislation desired. The power of appointments, alone, is
such a great one that, with it, any President might
subvert and overthrow well-established institutions.
The Senate was expressly provided as a check upon
this power. The President has the right to select, and
the Senate has the equal right to reject. In the same
way, the President has his check upon the legislation
of Congress. He has the right of veto, and it takes a
two-thirds vote to go beyond this adverse action.

Senators are very proud of their privileges, and
watch, with jealous care, to guard against any en-
croachments upon their rights. Each senator represents the influence and power of a sovereign State.
He is looked up to, in his State, as a leader, by the
great mass of voters, without any regard to the current criticisms of the time. A President, who need-
lessly offends a senator in the selection of appointments, is not a statesman, much less a politician ; for he
provokes endless conflicts, antagonizes the powerful
Senate, and renders impracticable the best-laid plans
for his own administration.

So it can be seen how this second affront came with
the same conspicuous effect as a resounding slap on the
face of Senator Norton. He affected indifference ; but,
as he glanced up at the gallery to note the effect upon

the correspondents assembled there, his glance met
mine. He frowned slightly, as much as to say : " Do you
now understand what I expect of you ?   Is it not time
for a counter-blow ? "

I ran out of the gallery, fearing he might send for
me, and hastened up town to the hotel, to see Captain
Harcourt.

CHAPTER X.

THE LADY IN THE CASE.

As I came up on the sidewalk, in front of the Arlington Hotel, I noticed a carriage stopping in front of the awning-covered entrance for ladies. As I crossed directly under it, I observed the wife of my friend, the Cabinet officer. The moment she saw me she hastily beckoned me to the carriage door. I never saw her looking better than in this hour of her danger. Did she know how her brilliant position was even now being threatened? In many ways she was a wonderful and admirable woman, who deserved a better fate.

Sylvia Granger, as she beckoned me to her side, deserves a brief description, as she was then one of the great powers, in not only the social world, but the political, as well. Although born in the far West, she was of sturdy Puritan stock. This element gave her intellectual superiority and clear common sense, while her Western life and education had given her a breadth of view and a dash, which made her an engaging companion. At the time of my story, she was in the neighborhood of thirty-five years of age. She was tall, dark, and with the slim figure of a girl. She was always dressed richly, but with only occasional suggestions of brilliancy, appearing in the simple key of colors employed in her toilettes.

Black was her favorite color, as it so well set off her clear, olive complexion. She had the simplicity and directness of a man accustomed to large affairs, and in no way employed the small affectations common to her sex. Yet she had a wonderful fascination over men. Without apparent effort, she had in her train half of the public men in Washington. Upon her reception days her house was crowded with the best people. Her dinners were most eagerly sought after. Her world, in the main, was political, and she understood politics so well that she talked but little on the subject, and, when with the public men of the day, understood how to listen. But, when it came to the movements of a political intrigue, there was no one so active and powerful in gathering about her the elements to control or overwhelm an opposition. She was a great favorite with the President on account of her brilliancy, her beauty, and her shrewdness. Mrs. Granger loved power, and her ambition knew but few limits. If she could have had great wealth at her command, she would never have taken any but safe paths ; but, not having it, and having risen so rapidly, her needs and wants had descended upon her like a devouring host, that had to be met some way. She had so many rivals, and they were all so pitiless. The atmosphere of excitement in which she lived was not conducive to reflection. So, when an opportunity was afforded to make some money in exchange for the wielding by her of a certain influence in the distribution of the patronage of her husband's department, she did not hesitate. If she had not been in such great need, and

if the offer had not come in such an insidious, indirect
way, she would have, perhaps, had time to see the
danger of her act, and its possible ruin of her husband.
At the bottom, she believed herself a good woman.
Her ambition centered upon her husband. She wished
to see him President of the United States, and daily
exerted her brilliant powers to make him friends. She
used to love him, and still respected and honored him.
Later, when times were quieter, she might again love
him; but, in the drive of occupation of each, the two
were absorbed, and met, at intervals, in their busy days,
as friends, who had certain interests in common. Their
three children, two daughters and a son, were in school.
The daughters were in the convent at Georgetown,
while the boy was in a private school preparing for ad-
mission to the Naval Academy.

Secretary Granger was a friend of mine long before
he became the favorite adviser of the President of the
United States. In his advancement, he never changed
his attitude towards me. The intimacy of early years
was increased, if anything, as he rose to power.

Mrs. Granger, as she beckoned to me to approach,
without reply to my salutation of polite inquiry concerning her health, asked me, abruptly, if I had any
engagement for the next hour or so; "For," said she,
with a smile, anticipating my reply, "I want you to
come with me. I am out paying calls, and, if you will
enter the carriage, I will have a chance to talk with
you, as I shall go in at very few places, perhaps none.
Can you come?"

I looked at Mrs. Granger, as I replied that nothing

would give me greater pleasure. It was the first
special notice I had had from her. She had always
treated me well, as her husband's friend. Why this
attention? Did she know anything? If she did, there
was no betrayal of it in her manner. She looked as
fresh and bright, in the clear, soft air of that bright,
winter morning, as if there was no such thing as care
in the world. She wore, upon her blue-black hair, a
tiny bonnet of black lace. Dark furs and robes en-
veloped her. At her throat, where the circle of sable
parted, there was a touch of scarlet, that encircled her
graceful throat, a line of color against the dark shade
of her walking dress. A great bunch of English violets,
pinned upon her breast, filled the dark brougham
with the perfume of a hothouse. She tugged, with
impatience, at the carriage door, to open it, as I was
bowing my acceptance ; and before I could give my assistance, and before the correct footman had begun to
unbend to descend for orders, the carriage door was
opened, and I was, in a moment, seated in one corner,
under the furs, with the most fascinating, self-willed,
and independent woman in Washington society. The
spirited pair of blacks attached to the carriage sprang
away at the sound of the closing door.

"Now we can talk undisturbed," said my companion.
"The footman has the list and the cards, so I need to
pay no attention to that. Now, in politics and the
modern school of diplomacy, the rules say it is best to
be simple and direct. I want your advice and help in
a matter that greatly concerns my husband."

"Your husband?"

"Yes; my husband. You have relations with Senator Norton. I hear that you were with him last night, after leaving the Russian Legation. How did I hear? Oh, never mind. How does one hear everything in Washington, where secrets fly about on wings? Now, I do not propose to press you for any details of that interview; but I know that Senator Norton is vigorously plotting a savage attack upon the President, and that this attack is to be made through my husband. Am I well informed?"

"You are."

"The nature of the attack, alone, I do not know. That is the only thing that puzzles me. My husband, as you know, is the soul of honor. He is too honorable for a successful fighter with such a man as Norton; but I have heard several times, within the last twenty-four hours, from friends of mine in the Senate, that my husband was in danger. So greatly impressed have I been with the correctness of this information, that I went to the President yesterday, after the Cabinet meeting, to ask him to suspend all action against Senator Norton until the situation is cleared. But you know the President. He is obstinate, combative, and not over clear of vision. His entire object in life, at present, is to humiliate Senator Norton, and he does not believe the latter can retaliate in any way that will amount to anything."

"What do you think?"

"I think this—that Senator Norton is not a man to boast idly. He could not restrain himself, the other evening, when talking to the wife of Justice Black,

who greatly admires him. He more than hinted that
my husband was soon to come a cropper, and, of
course, she told me. She even said that there was a
combination made to drive him out of the Cabinet,
which could not fail to succeed. That is absurd, of
course. But, in all the fights we have been through,
I have never had such an impression of weight and
directness as in the present case. I have tried to warn
the President, but you know how difficult it is to
change him."

"Have you heard of the nomination he sent in
to-day?"

"Blovis for the Berlin mission? Has the name
actually gone in?"

"It has."

"I knew it was probable. But I had hoped it would
be delayed. The President is there in error, and proceeds against the advice of his Cabinet. To push
Senator Norton too far will create public sympathy
for him and unpopularity for the President. Now, do
you know the line of attack proposed?"

"I do."

At this, Mrs. Granger faced about, and, for the first
time, her face paled. Nervously locking her hands
together, she said, in a quiet, repressed manner of intense attention: "Tell me all about it."

"How can I?"

"How can you refuse, and call yourself my husband's
friend?"

"Still, it is a most difficult thing to tell."

"Ah"—her woman's intuition was beginning to

divine why I hesitated—"do you hesitate to talk on account of the nature of the attack? Is it anything you should conceal from me, a something that loyal men never tell to the wives of their best friends?"

"No; it is not that; and no one should know that better than you."

"What is it?"

At this, the carriage stopped at a residence next to the Granger house. It was the Austrian Legation. As the footman was ringing the bell, there came a tap upon the carriage window, and then the sound of girlish laughter. There stood, upon the sidewalk, Mrs. Granger's two daughters, one twelve and the other fourteen, in the company of a discreet Sister. The two girls were just leaving the house for a return to the school. They were delighted to meet their mother on their road, and they came flying to her carriage, chattering and laughing, as they burst in upon her, to hug her, and to lay at her feet their ardent worship. These gracious American princesses—one a blonde and the other a dark-eyed, black-haired madcap, the very image of her mother—were alive with health and fun. They passed on in a moment, but the sight of them gave my thoughts another turn. I had been growing hard in my judgment of the Cabinet officer's wife, who I knew to be responsible for all this complication in which her husband was being involved. But, as I witnessed the scene between the mother and her children, I relented. At best, it is hard to be judicial in passing upon the faults of very handsome women. With ugly ones, we can mete out justice with an unsparing hand.

But to be anything but lenient with such a woman, now seemed, to me, to be impossible.

As the carriage moved on, Mrs. Granger was silent for a moment, and then she began: "You had better tell me. I shall know, in any event. So what is the difference?"

"Let me ask you, first, a question, and you must promise not to be offended."

"Offended! Not possible!"

"Yes; it may be possible. Let me ask you to look over your own career in Washington. Have you always been careful to do nothing that would give the enemies of your husband an advantage?"

The eyes of my companion flashed, as I hastened to add: "Pardon me. You ask me to talk plainly. It is only in that way I can aid you. Have you always been careful, as has been your husband, in guarding against acts that could be misconstrued?"

Still Mrs. Granger said nothing, but looked at me with the careful, intense look of one facing a deadly attack.

I continued: "I do not love beating about. Senator Norton has in his hands certain papers relating to the award of the Warner contracts. Why did you allow your stupid, contractor cousin, Brown, to be so prominent in this, as an intermediary? He has signed receipts, and written enough compromising letters, concerning this affair, to ruin forty good men. It makes no difference how innocent you are; it will all come home to you and, in the end, to your husband."

Mrs. Granger, for the moment, was overwhelmed.

She sank back blank, pale and nerveless. The source of the attack had been so unexpected. From the silence and extreme pallor, I could judge how the blow had struck home. Suddenly, the carriage stopped. We were now upon the brow of Capitol Hill, facing the splendid marble pile of the Capitol, shining white in the bright rays of a brilliant, sunny afternoon. Up the winding roadway, under the marble terrace, upon the side of the Senate wing, there came the simple, but imposing pageant of a military funeral, which, for the moment, barred our path.

The wailing bugles, the muffled drum beats, accompanying this last march of some unknown, military hero, filled the air with sadness. Some cadence of this song of grief pierced through the shield of reserve of this woman of the world, and she burst into a perfect passion of weeping.

This breakdown was but for a moment. The worst now being known, Mrs. Granger soon raised her head and resumed something of the self-possession of her former manner, although she was dreadfully shaken, as I could see by the involuntary trembling of the tips of her fingers, notwithstanding the apparent control of her face. The trembling of her fingers touched me more than would the wildest cries of agony, and I then and there became her champion—resolved to defend her, regardless of any abstract question of right or wrong.

Finally, I told her what I had already done. When I described my interview with General Starr, her face lighted for the first time. "He is a brave, true, old

man," said she, "and as wise as he is brave. Will you see
me as soon as you have come from him this evening?"

"Gladly, but where?"

"I am to be at a dinner at the British Legation this
evening. After, I am one of the chaperons at the
Assembly. You will find me there until two o'clock
in the morning. Then I shall go home."

"Senator Norton will surely wish to see me this
evening."

"You will have time for that. I should prefer that
you learn all you can before coming to me."

"General Starr may go to the President after going
over the case, at ten o'clock, at his house."

"Well, well; I must be patient as I can. Keep all
this from my husband, if it can be done; but can it be
done?" Here the hands began to tremble again.

"It is a miserable affair, but you must not worry or
lose your courage for a moment."

"It is easy to have courage when one is right; but,
in this, I have been so hopelessly in the wrong. What
must you think of me?"

"I am not in this case to pass judgment upon any
one. I am ready, as a loyal friend, to act with my
eyes shut, and will leave the ethics of the situation to
be discussed by our enemies."

"Our enemies. Thank you."

A few minutes later, Mrs. Granger said she must now
dismiss me. She did not make the mistake of trying to
defend herself. She only said: "I shall not lessen
your sympathies by trying, in any way, to exculpate
myself. In this affair I have been wofully wrong, and

am inexcusably guilty. My cousin is not really the
responsible one. If my needs had not been so great I
would not, perhaps, have been so stupidly remiss. I have
failed as the guardian of my husband's honor. In my
carelessness I have thought mere bodily purity compre-
hended all my duty concerning him. How complete is my
failure, I understand better than any one else. If I could
take the burden of this upon my own shoulders, I should
have more courage. But I cannot. Life is too complicated in its relations for any one to be able to do that."

Her simple courage, and the directness with which
she admitted the full extent of her misstep, increased my
admiration for her. As I descended from her carriage,
in front of my hotel, I pressed her hands with fervor.

"Count on me, and trust me," I said, with the en-
thusiasm of a deep emotion of pity.

As I spoke, the thunderous hoof-beats of a horse,
ridden at high speed over the now partially cleared
asphalt, caused me to turn my head. The rider was
Senator Norton, and he smiled with satirical satisfaction
as he gravely saluted me, while yet I was bidding farewell to Mrs. Granger.

The Senator had resumed his afternoon rides. When
he had any political fight on hand of unusual importance he went, at once, into physical training. His
presence in the open air, upon the back of his favorite
horse, was an advertisement to the watchful world of
Washington that the powerful Senator had just thrown
down the gauntlet to some redoubtable antagonist,
and was preparing a full stock of physical strength for
a period of excitement and struggle.

CHAPTER XI.

GENERAL STARR IS INVITED TO TAKE PART IN THE FIGHT AS A PEACE-MAKER.

It was in the middle of the afternoon, when I returned to the hotel. I immediately sought the dining-room, for my lunch; as I had now so many engagements ahead of me for the next twelve hours, I needed my full strength. First, I was to see Captain Harcourt for special advice and conference, as a preliminary to a very busy evening. It was almost certain, that Senator Norton would send for me. I was to call upon General Starr at ten o'clock, and I felt sure he would go at once to the President afterward. He would not leave the White House before midnight, and then I would have to hurry to the Assembly rooms to find Mrs. Granger. After lunch I went to my room, resolving to stay there until dinner-time, and not call upon Captain Harcourt until evening. I partially undressed and lay down for a nap. In this sleep I had a strange dream. I thought that I met my soul, who said to me: "At last we are becoming acquainted. The more you sympathize with the suffering of others, and the harder you work to lessen their pain, the nearer we come together." Then the dream faded and I slept profoundly.

It was late when I awoke. I dressed carefully for the evening before going down to dinner, and when

once in the dining-room, I looked about for Captain
Harcourt. But he had already dined. I found him in
his favorite seat in the center of the hotel office. As I
took a seat by his side, I felt, without one word of
greeting from him, his intense sympathy, and knew in
some intangible way, that if all else failed, I could
rely upon him. After recounting to him, briefly, my
experiences of the day, I asked him if he had any
further advice or suggestions.

"Not now. Come to my rooms after you have
finished with your visits of the night. We will then go
over, carefully, the facts of the situation. We will first
look at them long, then exactly as they are, free from
all color, and then we will look at the reverse picture,
as a correction of its errors. You are now passing
through an experience which is of value to you, as it
will burn deep into your consciousness, the fact of the
false values of the life of the great American republic.
Here, at the National Capital, is the mainspring of our
life as a nation. If the science of government, the
greatest science left to be developed for the benefit of
man, is degraded to petty personal struggles of vindictive ambition, then the whole nation must, in the end,
feel the effect of such degradation. You stand this
evening under the shadow of a cruel tragedy brought
about by the selfish striving of the intense rivalry of
modern political and social life. Can you do anything? Is it wise to suppress the climax of the disaster?
This outbreak, in which your personal sympathies are
enlisted, assumes on that account an overshadowing
importance. May there not be some development,

equally cruel, in another quarter, springing from the same cause, but which may leave your personal sympathies untouched?"

"Then you do not propose to really help me?" I was stung by his philosophical calmness.

"I did not say so. I shall help you, but perhaps not in the way you may wish. You may not be the best judge of what is help."

Our conversation was interrupted here by a messenger, who came to tell me that Senator Norton would like to see me a moment. I hesitated a moment, thinking whether it would be best to plead some engagement, when the messenger, who was the Senator's confidential body servant, added that his master had directed him to say that, if I was very busy, any time before twelve o'clock the next day would do as well.

I turned to Captain Harcourt. "Go and see him," said he, "call there on your way to General Starr's."

I whispered a brief message to the servant, and then I went to order a hansom cab for the evening. It was now nine o'clock and I left the hotel at once, leaving Captain Harcourt at his post of observer of the ever-changing groups that came and went through the hotel.

I drove to the Hotel Jefferson and was shown up to Senator Norton's rooms. I found his drawing-room filled with men. His followers in the delegation in the House were all present. Here and there were to be found Norton's closest allies in the Senate chamber, every one of whom cordially hated the President on account of some disappointment at his hands. Cham-

pagne bottles were placed upon every available object
of support in the room. Blue clouds of smoke filled
the air, overcoming with its pungent odor the heavy
perfumes of the flowers that were always to be found
in the Senator's quarters. The conversation in the
room rose and fell with the roar of passion and excitement. What subtle poison of excitement there is
to be found in every political contest! The men who
met here, to talk and sympathize with the Senator,
were as angry as so many feudal barons, whose rights
were threatened by some usurper.

Senator Norton dominated the assemblage. He
moved about from one group to the other, barely tast-
ing the freely-flowing wine and not lighting the cigar
that he crushed between his even, white, strong teeth.

He hurried me to a private room, away from the
crowd. He locked the door and then turned to me as
he said: "Have you anything to tell me?"

"No; not yet."

"I wanted to tell you one thing. I gave you forty-
eight hours. You have all the facts, and the permission to use them. I do not want you to send the story,
even if you decide to use it, before seeing me. You
have no intention to send anything to-night?"

"No; I have no such intention."

"Good; that is all I wished to say."

The Senator was not a man given to repeating dramatic effects. He had said to me all he had intended,
the night before. I knew his intentions regarding
the President. There was no need of his making any
allusion to the second blow of the President, delivered

that day. His request, or rather his command, merely confirmed the view General Starr had taken of the case, and so it was with a lighter heart that I left the hotel, and buttoned my ulster about me, as I directed the cab to be driven to General Starr's house, which was perched upon the heights of Kalorama, some two miles distant. It was a clear night, and over the smooth asphalt we made very good time. I rang the bell at the Senator's house, just as my watch marked ten o'clock.

I was shown in by a tall negro butler, in plain evening dress, instead of the livery affected in the average senatorial household. He copied the grim gravity of his master.

I was ushered into a huge library sitting-room, filled along its walls with shelf upon shelf of books and pamphlets. In every opening possible were portraits of military heroes ; military emblems and flags were the principal adornments of this huge room. In the center was a large, open fire-place, upon which blazed sputtering logs of wood. In front of the fire, upon a crimson rug, lay two dogs, one a brown Irish setter, the other a full-blood Newfoundland dog of fine breed. The General, in evening dress, sat in a strong, oaken chair, at the left of the fire, puffing at his eternal cigar. Upon his further left were two secretaries, drudging away at the letters indicated in the morning conference at the Committee Room at the Capitol. It was the General's favorite reception hour, and, as he sat with a host of callers about him, he well deserves a picture, for he was one of the most unique characters who ever filled high public place. He was then sixty years of age. His figure was slight, but above the medium height, with the lines of muscular vigor of a man of surpassing strength. His once dark hair had turned to a soft yellow-white, which stood up in irregular spiky masses over his square, high forehead. His eyes, a piercing blue-gray in repose, were peaceful, but, in the excitement of battle, fairly blazed with an unholy light. His nose was straight and his mouth large, full and stern. It was shaded by a drooping, long, gray mustache, falling, in sweeping, careless ends, upon his square pugnacious, powerful chin. His jaws were blue from the heavy roots of the smoothly cut beard, against the clear brown of his weather-tanned face. His voice, in ordinary speech, was slow and drawling; but, when excited or angry, it was a deep, powerful bass. His feet and hands might have excited the envy of a lady, so small and gracefully formed were they. He was a man incapable of betraying a trust, or in failing to come to the support of a friend. He loved a fight as a drunkard loves wine. but he never sought a quarrel with any one. His honesty was so unquestioned, that no enemy, in the most bitter of the mud-throwing of political contests, had ever thought or dared to question it. Underneath a mask of stern indifference he carried a heart of exquisite tenderness. But with all his calm, he was subject to occasional bursts of temper, during which he spoke with a tongue of fury, and sputtered oaths, with the volubility of a soldier of the old school; yet, he was a profoundly religious man, and always stood ready to knock any Christian down, who dared to disagree with him upon a question of theology.

In the group about General Starr, at the time of my call, were to be seen the leading types of the floating life of Washington. No one, who wanted to see General Starr, was ever refused admittance to the light and warmth of his library, where he sat in a kind of solemn state and listened to the numerous petitions that were presented for his consideration. Beggars, even, were to be found in the crowd. All were welcome, although those who had no real claim upon his attention never got very far. The General, during these hours of daily reception of the lame, halt and blind of Washington politics, was generally very silent. He looked straight into the fire and smoked. He listened to the longest stories, without a trace of weariness. Perhaps he did not always listen, but he had the appearance of it. No one was ever told to go, and it was always midnight before the last caller was gone. If the General wished to go out, his overcoat would be brought to him by some attendant, and out he would go, without a word or a salute. If the company wished to wait his return and warm their toes at his open fire, they were welcome—only no one must interfere with the work of the secretaries, who worked with feverish energy to catch up with the long letter list. For the Senator would answer every letter sent him, and, this being well known, the letters seeking his help came to him in clouds from all over the United States.

He nodded at me as I entered, and pointed with a thumb to a chair near him, a chair never occupied by any of his visitors, except upon his special invitation. He then handed me a cigar—another mark of favor—and then looked at me as the next man entitled to speak. I told him, in a low voice, just what I had done during the day, of my talk with Sylvia, and the importance of the testimony obtained from her of the absolute innocence of her husband.

The General smoked, as I talked, but said nothing. I was, however, used to his ways, and was content to wait.

Just as I had finished talking, the wife of the General, a handsome woman, near the age of her husband, but alive and alert with the energy of youth, came into the room with her two daughters, both married, prominent as handsome, well-bred women, who knew every one, and who were welcome for their brightness and good nature more than for their elegance of dress. They were all dressed to go, and called upon the General to accompany them.

He stood up with alacrity, as he said: "You will have to excuse me now. Go ahead! I may join you at the Legation. If I don't, you will have to do your rounds alone to-night. I am going to the White House to see the President, and the Assembly, where you are going, will be too late for me."

When the General spoke, there was nothing more to be said. There was a moment of hurried talk and salutation with those in the library who were known to them, and then the ladies passed out.

The General went with me to my cab, muffled in a huge, blue coat of army pattern; a soft, black hat was slouched down over his face. When we were once under way, with directions given to go direct to the White House, the General's jaws were loosed. For the first five minutes, he passed in solemn review all of the most formal and blood-curdling oaths known to the language. Said he, after this necessary prelude: " This is nice business for an old man like me, to be running about on a cold winter's night, when I might be at home, by my fire: just because two obstinate, stiff-necked fools, who call themselves statesmen, want to quarrel, my God, about an office. Because of this quarrel, a family is to be stabbed to death, with the dagger of scandal, because a woman has committed a sin. Now, the time that it is necessary to take up to head off this tragedy, inspired and driven on by the cruel and selfish vanity of two men, is enough to drive a man to drink."

The Senator continued in this strain until the cab dashed through the iron gates of the White House grounds, up to the very entrance, between the blazing lights that illuminated the old-fashioned, high portico of the Executive Mansion.

I no longer recognized my friend. The Oriental calm of the man of peace had given way for the fire and fury of the soldier, who had led the fiercest charges of the war, and who, during four years of almost continuous fighting, had never once turned his back upon the enemy.

CHAPTER XII.

AN AFTER MIDNIGHT RECEPTION AT THE WHITE HOUSE.

The lower part of the White House was lighted, while the private wing was brilliantly illuminated. The President, at that time, held many conferences after midnight. It was the best time for his intimates to reach him. It was during these morning hours that some of the most important acts of his administration were planned. The policeman, in plain clothes, at the door opened, after we had rung once or twice, and instantly admitted us the moment he saw General Starr. It was the first time I had crossed the threshold of the White House at this hour. The General asked to have his name sent up, saying that he wished to see the President upon a matter of unusual importance. We were shown up-stairs, and left to wait in the long, narrow room where the Cabinet meetings were generally held.

After ten minutes had passed, another attendant came to us, and ushered us directly into the private conference room of the President, where a light repast was being served. This long, oval room was ablaze with light and good cheer. The table was covered with delicacies of a very substantial character. Cold pastries, flanked with potted birds, and a great pigeon-pie, near the President's elbow, showed signs of attack of the most vigorous character. Magnums of champagne stood about in careless, inviting attitudes. A round dozen of the President's familiars were about the table, stuffing, drinking, smoking and talking, all at the same time. In the group were three or four of the administration leaders in the Senate, several members of the House who were in the President's confidence, and three or four members of that mysterious body known as the Kitchen Cabinet. These were rotund, well-groomed men, who looked as if the best of everything was none too good for them, and who had no special character or residence that was known to any one. They were simply known as the President's intimate friends and cronies. Where they came from; who they really were; what would become of them after the President should pass from power, were questions no one felt equal to answering.

The tone of the company was highly congratulatory. The President, flushed with good cheer and much flattering from his associates—and few Presidents hear anything but flattery—was in an exuberantly good humor. He waved his napkin cheerfully at General Starr, whom he liked very much, then pulled himself together with a slight frown when he saw me following at the General's heels. The President was not over-fond of newspaper correspondents, and never saw them outside of office hours. In this visit, however, I came not in my official capacity, but as a friend of General Starr's, and so the President, after bowing very coldly in my direction, asked General Starr to take a seat by his side and help himself to pigeon-pie. The members of the Kitchen Cabinet were very diplomatic people. They are very fond of newspaper correspondents, and the moment they saw that the President even tolerated my presence, they became effusive, and one of the extra-energetic members found me a seat, and, in another moment, I, too, had a helping from the pigeon-pie, which was the dish of honor.

General Starr barely touched what was offered him ; then he began to talk directly to the President. I studied the President's face during the conversation. The look of comfort and satisfaction, which had been brought out by the exquisite flavor of the pigeon and his favorite brand of champagne, now gave way to a shadow of vexation, which soon reached dissatisfaction and impatience.

Suddenly, he rose from the table, and asked General Starr to follow him. They walked into the President's bed-room, and, a moment afterwards, a messenger came for me and asked me to join them. The President was now very much agitated. He cross-examined me with feverish energy concerning the case, and asked, over and over again, for me to describe Senator Norton's manner. He, even, asked me to repeat his very words, and went so far in his minute inquiries as to ask me to try and give the very tone of the utterance. After he had finished his examination, he asked me to leave him alone with General Starr, as he did not wish to discuss the facts presented to him, in my presence.

I returned to the guests assembled about the pigeon-pie. It was a quarter after one when General Starr came out. He did not look contented. I never knew any one who had less skill in concealing dissatisfaction than he. He bowed rather curtly to the assembly, and I followed him out quickly, for the time was now growing short for my appointment with Mrs. Granger at the Assembly rooms. The General was grimly silent, going down-stairs. When we were once in the cab, I directed the driver to go to the Assembly rooms, and the General said that he would go home with his people, who were, probably, still there; and, if they were not, it was understood that he should have my cab, and I was to find my way home the best I could. When we were under way, he said: "I am disappointed with the result of my visit to-night. The President is a very weak man, and his vanity has been so flattered since he has become President, it is hard to do anything with him. If he had known all the facts of the case, as presented to him this evening, he would not have sent in that second nomination. But, having once made it, he will not withdraw it, and he will make no concessions to Senator Norton, not even to save his Cabinet officer. When he made that resolution, I told him the whole story, and how much to blame Mrs. Granger was. This made him peevish and fretful. He said I had quite destroyed his digestion. It had ruined his supper. By God, sir, I think he thought more of losing the pleasure of the digestion of that pigeon-pie than any other fact connected with the case. Mrs. Granger is a great favorite of his. He, like all weak men, wants to temporize. He has great con-

fidence in Mrs. Granger's diplomatic abilities. He
believes that she will arrange this affair some way, and
has sent for her to come to the White House to-morrow
morning to see him. I don't think he cares two
straws about what she has done. As he said to me,
with a smile : 'Women have no real idea of business,
and what would be high crime in a man, in such a
matter, was an ordinary peccadillo in a woman.' He
has no loyalty of character, and would sacrifice
Granger to-morrow, in a moment, if he could do it
without scandal, rather than make the slightest concession to Norton. His massive brain is, at present,
permeated with the thought that he is standing on a
principle, and that the affair is one which concerns the
dignity of his office. He is on such high ground, the
devil could not touch him with an argument ; and any
appeal to him, upon the ground of sympathy or kindness, is worse than a waste of breath. He scoffs at the
idea of any tragic possibilities, and had the calm assurance to tell me that I was too innocent for political
life, and that I took things altogether too seriously.
Still, with all his lightness of character, and his fond-
ness for being amused, he will wake up to-morrow
morning very grave and serious. I can't do anything
more to-night. I shall, probably, see Norton myself
to-morrow. I am going to play a square game with
him. I shall tell him exactly all the story that relates
to Mrs. Granger. I do not believe that Norton would
want to push any woman to the wall. If it can be
made clear that it is the woman that is bound to be
sacrificed, I may make Norton hesitate ; but, if the

President does not make some kind of concession, he will be as relentless as an Indian when on the track of his revenge, and he will, undoubtedly, assume, knowing Granger as he does, that he will come to the front and bear the burden of the whole thing, and that Mrs. Granger, in reality, will not be hurt. Of course, he does not really understand her character. I do not believe she is the kind of woman who will sit back with her mouth shut, and see her husband's honor sacrificed. But, then, the devil of it is, there are the children. What can she do? Poor girl! I knew her when she was a baby, and have seen her grow up and develop, and reach success she deserved. The trouble, at the last, has been her ambition."

We were now at the Assembly rooms. A broad blaze of light came out from the hallway, filled with plants and flowers, through which ran a broad strip of carpeting out over the steps and across the sidewalk. Soldiers in uniform stood about as guards of honor, for the Assembly that night was under military direction. The great windows of the Masonic Temple, where the cotillion was conducted, were filled with flags and lights. Up the stairways we marched, meeting and saluting occasional groups of departing guests from among the spectators; but the members of the Assembly were all faithful to their leader, and, from their ranks, not one had departed when we entered the floor. The vibrating floor, the undulating movement of the throng of dancers, the wild music of the stringed band of the Marine Corps, appealed to our senses of sight and hearing, as we entered the door. We stood there a moment, watching the winding in and out of the fanciful figures, and then the General found his people, or, rather, they came to him. A moment later, I was alone. I had not gone far about the room, when Mrs. Granger passed, leaning upon the arm of the German Minister, on her way to the door. She saluted me, gravely, as I passed ; and then I turned and followed her, without having the appearance of being specially interested. At the hall, I delayed a moment, and then passed out, and reached the sidewalk just as the minister had made his most profound salutations to Mrs. Granger at the carriage door.

I advanced, in my turn, and had a chance only to whisper a word. "There is, really, no news; nothing decisive has been done." Then I told her, in a word, about our visit to the White House, and that the President was going to send for her in the morning. This last piece of news gave her a shock. "The President is going to send for me?" she said.

"Yes," said I ; " he thinks that you, yourself, should be the one to manage this affair."

All this took less than a moment, and she thanked me for my devotion to her interests during the day, and begged me to come and lunch at her house the next day. Her carriage now moved on, and I walked home to my hotel, where I found a message in my box from Captain Harcourt, asking me to come to his rooms the moment I should return, no matter how late the hour.

CHAPTER XIII.

I AM INTRODUCED AT LAST TO MY IMMORTAL SOUL.

Had it not been for the experience with Captain Harcourt in his rooms, upon my return from the Assembly meeting, it is doubtful whether I should have made any attempt to write an account of my experiences in Washington during this eventful winter; for there was not enough of the unusual in the intrigue developed between the President and Senator Norton to warrant my putting it together in permanent form. I had been through many similar experiences, where, as a disinterested spectator, I had been privileged, by my profession, to watch the play from behind the scenes. But, in this affair, there was at last the note of absorbing personal interest, engaged through my friendship and affection for the people most seriously threatened, and so the experience I was now undergoing became so unique as to make a permanent influence on my life. This influence was deepened and completed by Captain Harcourt, so that what, at first, merely promised to be a prominent chapter in my life's career, became, as a matter of fact, the one dominating division of my history, marking a change as great as if death had kindly moved me onward into another world.

When I entered Captain Harcourt's sitting-room, after reading his message in the hotel office below, I was weary with my long and fatiguing day. Hardly had I crossed the threshold of the room, however, when my fatigue fell away like a cloak, and an unusual sense of freshness and vigor came to me.

Captain Harcourt was in his favorite lounging attitude of observant expectancy. He gently signed to me to take a seat opposite, and, for a few moments, there was silence between us. I was now conscious of a new feeling in his presence. He no longer seemed to be my refined and philosophical every-day friend; rather a superior, who now had summoned me before him for admonition and judgment; but, yet, whatever the admonition or judgment, I accepted it implicitly in advance, so pure and all-pervading was the spirit of gentleness and kindness that transfigured his plain-featured face.

In other ways, there appeared to be a great change in the room since I had last seen it. The ordinary and conventional adornments of the chamber had disappeared. The walls were concealed behind masses of dark, Oriental tapestries, threaded here and there with colors so brilliant as to shine, by contrast, like the gleam of jewels. There was a faint odor of some unknown perfume in the air that soothed the wearied sense like a gentle touch of a loving hand. The light in the room was glowing soft, but yet, steadily brilliant, without a second of wavering. As I sat, looking absently, but contentedly, at Captain Harcourt, there came to my surprised and delighted ear the sounds of distant harmonics, which rose and fell like waves of a mighty sea. Was it the effect of my imagination, stimulated by my physical fatigue? This was the question I asked myself over and over again.

"No," replied Captain Harcourt to my silent inquiry; "it is not the effect of your imagination, but, simply, by an enlargement of your powers to see and hear. You are now, at last, in the atmosphere and surroundings of your own soul."

"My soul! What has that to do with the apparent change in the surroundings of this room?"

"It has all that there is to do with it," answered my companion. "Within every man there dwells a portion of divinity, capable of leading him to the highest pleasures and highest possibility. It is this element which makes all men absolutely equal, and the apparent inequalities existing, exist only because of the inequality of results obtained in reaching up to this high being, who stands patient through the centuries of trial, until the spirit receives his pure embrace, and perfection becomes the result."

"Do you mean that you, by your conscious association with your own soul, have at last arrived at a condition of perfection?"

"By no means. But I have so clearly before me the standard, that I am less anxious to err. My natural inclination and pleasure lie in the direction of his pure and peaceful companionship. But the inherited habits of the past are still at war within me. My one great danger lies in inaction, in listening too long to the sweet harmonies of the Universe, and to my closing my

ears and eyes against the discords and cruelties of ordinary life."

I thought of his apparent indifference to the possible disgrace of my dearest and most valued friend, and
was about to speak, when he said : " In that you mis-
judge me. I have not been indifferent to what has
caused so much pain and trouble : but my knowledge
does not give me the authority or power to change the
order of existing things. I possess no magic wand,
through the gift of being able to see more clearly my
surroundings : though, in the end, such knowledge,
widely diffused, will change the entire character of
the life of the world as it is now lived."

" Is this development, through you, a new departure
of a higher civilization ? "

" No ; at long intervals, men have been endowed with
rare gifts for self-communion, and then history records
of them the acts of the leaders who have moved the
world. It has given the martyrs of the past their tranquility under the fiercest of tortures. For who can
torture the soul ? The man who comes into close
inter-communion with his higher self is beyond the
range of earthly power. Every great thing in life
comes from soul development. Every inspiration of
the poet, the artist, the musician, is the record of the
higher self, who is always pure, true and perfect in all
things. When the thread of communion is kept perfect, the result is the wonder of the world, and the
story of such inspiration goes down through the ages
as part of divine history."

" Do you mean by that to refer to the Christ story ? "

" Just that.   Jesus Christ is the one and only man who has lived upon this earth entirely in harmony and in full accord with the divine part of him—his soul.   He knew his soul as no one since has ever known him ; and the true and correct story of his life, stripped of all idle superstition and legend, will show just that. Through his complete assimilation to the perfect condition of his soul he reached the full limits of the higher existence in this world, within the span of a single life, so that he will need never return—in fact cannot return here—until entire humanity upon the earth has risen to the standard created by his life."

" Does Doctor Longman, upon the Island of Nolos, really represent the spirit of the Christ movement ? "

" It is the same influence, but acting under different conditions, suitable to the growth and education of the world.   We have outgrown the age of simplicity, and the shell of selfishness and indifference that has always ruled and controlled the mass of the world is to be attacked in another way."

" Why is it—if every man contains within himself the means of perfect contentment and happiness—that the source of such happiness is kept hidden from him? Why is not every man given a chance to rise to the highest powers of his capacity? "

" Every man is given the chance.   But with the law of free will, under which the race of this earth has been developed, no man can be forced in the direction of either evil or good.   He is allowed to follow his own inclination."

" But how can you explain that the inclination of

nearly every one is not towards the good? Why does not the divine portion, which dwells within, as you say, have a greater influence?"

"It is the spirit that is ever separate from the soul, until perfection is reached, that controls the seat of intelligence, where is germinated the base of every action."

"But, if the spirit controls, what becomes of free will of the man himself? He is but a tool in the hands of a spirit."

"Not so. The spirit is all that there is to man. It dwells within the inner citadel of the life principle, and to all essential purposes is man himself. It flashes the messages to the brain, which is a mere instrument for the expression of the will of the spirit. When the spirit departs, the brain and all its intricate machinery, controlling so-called human action, falls, an inert mass. The spirit is the interpreter of the soul, and, through its success or failure in this regard, marks the character of the man as he moves in the world here below."

"Does the spirit see clearly?"

"Not always. If it did, human development would be much more rapid."

"Is it through a succession of existences that the spirit finally rises to perfect union with the soul?"

"It is through such means alone that the spirit finally rises."

"But how can there be a gain through a succession of existences, when we retain no consciousness nor memory of previous existences?"

"If memory were given, then the free will of the

spirit would be fettered. As it is, the spirit rarely retrogrades. There is always a slight advance. It is like the creation of a planet. Time does not count. If a hundred million of years are passed in the creation and development of the mere material elements of a sphere in the Universe, can you wonder at the slow development of the human race from the level of animalism to the height of divinity. You might seek to question the wisdom of creation, by asking why man should have been created imperfect; but the answer to that will be found in the history of every living thing. From imperfection and low development every thing of worth has come. It is the up-moving scale of existence that is established in accord with divine law. You might ask, with equal propriety, why are not planets launched full, completed, blooming, into perfection of existence, instead of becoming creatures of a mighty evolution, starting from a center of fiery and furious gases. Such questions cannot, however, reach to the dignity of criticism. We are all parts of an endless chain of development. Such development can be hastened by individual acts—by following the law which controls that development. The world, through all ages, has been subject to tidal waves of emotion or feeling, that have played the most important part in the history of the development of the race. Sometimes this has been through some long and cruel war; through some series of frightful oppressions, that has awakened the dormant sense of justice among the most cruelly indifferent; through some tide of sentiment, that has, through reformation, changed the entire character of the world in its wide-reaching effects. Such a movement is now impending. One of its main stations of direction is upon the Island of Nolos; while this country will be the theatre of its most active demonstration."

"Why has this country been selected?"

"The movement will be felt in all so-called civilized countries; but its greatest activity and influence will be in the United States. No other country is more steeped in materialism and selfishness. It is here, where the crust of selfishness has been the thickest, that the volcanic fires of the new movement will burst forth with the greatest force and energy. Already, signs are multiplying of the coming change. The slight escape of steam through the surface that marks the approach of a volcanic eruption is to be seen in every direction. During the last few years, rich men actually have begun to study ways and means to do good with their money. The great gifts to the public, in the form of institutions of help, are coming forth with a generosity and a thoughtfulness unknown in history. Instead of leaving their gifts to be distributed after they are dead and gone, rich men are coming to regard their possessions as trusts, and try, during their lives, to discharge those trusts so as to merit the approval of their immortal souls—their only real guides and companions."

"But, why have you never spoken to me of this before?"

"Because you were not in harmony with your own soul. No one, who was as indifferent as you were when I first knew you, would have cared to listen to the message of a new propaganda. Still less could you have become a leader. But now——"

" Wherein have I changed?"

" I see you active, troubled, hard at work, trying to save some one else. You have dropped, for the time, all thoughts of yourself, and so you have earned the right to be introduced to your immortal soul."

" But, my dear Captain Harcourt, you honor me without sufficient reason. I do not want over-praise for a simple act of duty that any friend would perform."

" When one performs his duty, as you are now doing it, with fiery heat and furious energy, I repeat, you are fulfilling the higher law. I may never find you at such a high plane of personal effort again; and, while you are there, and before you have gone back to the routine indifference of your ordinary life, I propose to show you the actual features of your **better** and divine self."

" But how can this be done?"

" It is through no magic. This room has been fitted up, temporarily, as one of Doctor Longman's rooms, in the Island of Nolos. These hangings are from there. The entire furniture of the room belongs, for the time being, to him."

"And the music?"

" It is the echo of the harmonies always heard there."

Here the Captain said : " Look straight ahead and you will, for a time, see the visions that should be at the command of all."

Scarcely had he spoken, when all sense of physical

existence departed from me. All consciousness was
concentrated in the organ of vision, upon which, with
lightning-like rapidity, was photographed every act
and scene of my life. The walls of the room had now
disappeared, and through whirling mists came the
visions, disappearing instantly the second of their perfect development. I no longer had any consciousness
of time. The music that accompanied the swift changes
was continuous, most low and sad, wailing over mis-
deeds, which were many, only rising joyously as the
good came to the surface. I sat as under some spell
of enchantment; but I have never experienced so much
poignant misery, as I sat and watched the fast-flying
scenes of my life of pitiful striving.

I will not attempt to describe any of them. Let
their memory remain, only, to me, as my punishment.
At the close, there was a triumphant note to the music;
and then, when the harmony pealed the highest and
most triumphant, the cloud parted, and I saw sitting
before me—myself. Reclining in an easy chair, clothed
in the modern dress of travel, sat my exact counterpart.
Exact, did I say: exact only in general resemblance, in
every detail wholly different—but, yet, different in a way
hard to describe—while the whole was such an apparent
reproduction of my individuality. I can only explain
this difference by saying that in everything he was perfection. He was, apparently, my height, no taller or
shorter; but the proportions of his figure to this height
were mathematically correct. Every feature of the
face represented actual perfection of the type I represented. Where nature had just missed the mark with

me, here was the measure of perfection to mark the failure or imperfection. His complexion was transparent and pure, his eyes aglow with light and divine gentleness, his lips warm with color, parting to show teeth of dazzling whiteness, while the hair which clustered about his serene face was as fine as silk, lying in an irregular wavy mass around the face. The look of kindness, of sympathy, upon this face, appealed to the depth of my consciousness, and gave me a pleasure I had never known before. The intimate and sympathetic knowledge of my personality that shone in his face, marked the closeness of the tie that bound us together. Ah! here, at last, was a friend, tried and true, who could never fail me, who could never misunderstand me, and, however wretchedly I should fail, would never cease to love me. I do not fear the charge of egotism in my sudden worship of my higher self, for he was everything that I was not, and to praise him does not in any way commend myself.

It was a strange experience to sit opposite one's very image, and, yet, with such a consciousness of inferiority, as if one were in the presence of a God.

For a long time I could not speak, but sat and looked into the face of my inner self, visible to me for the first time. What an incentive to human action, to win the approval of such a lofty being! Involuntarily, I thought what sacrifices would I not make to please him. My mood found a reflex upon his face in a smile of the most gentle tenderness, and then I found courage to speak.

It was with halting phrase that I spoke. I had the

timidity and uncertainty of a child in the presence of one it both loved and feared. But, in a few moments, I was at my ease. Then the conversation opened—as such an one must, naturally, have begun—by a series of questions and answers. The hardest thing for me to realize was the assertion that this gracious and perfect being was part of me, and that he had always been. Only my blindness and ignorance had kept me from him. So I ventured, to make this assurance doubly certain, by asking :

" Have you always been with me ? "

" Always."

" And always will be ? "

" We cannot be separated. Our union is in accordance with divine law, which is fixed and immovable."

" Are you always willing to help me ? "

" More than willing. It is the chief object of my existence. In our union, perfect and complete, the advancement to other and better worlds alone can come."

" Am I to see you in the future as I see you now ? "

" It will depend upon yourself."

" Do you mean that I will, of my own volition, surrender the privilege of seeing and talking with my perfect self ? "

" It is more than possible."

" What could tempt me to give up such a priceless gift ? "

" Everything ; anything. The fixed habits of your life, as already made, are not to be broken lightly. You are now deeply moved. Communication between us is perfectly established ; but your spirit is not in real sympathy with me—in the sense that it will desire to continue the relations now so completely established. Your brain is a warehouse of impressions, long formed, which is opposed to me. Nearly every impression you will receive from life will be antagonistic to a belief in my existence, as you now know it. To-morrow, even, you will be inclined to look upon the experience of this night as a pleasant dream. In the absence of Captain Harcourt, it would not be difficult for you to explain to your satisfaction the occurrence of this evening, in accordance with your preconceived idea."

"Do you think so poorly of me?" As I said "of me" I thought of the complication of the double individuality. Which was the real I? Something of this I put in clumsy form.

"Your real individuality is in the spirit. It is the you that exists as you have always known yourself. I represent your future existence, when you have passed through the trials and experiences that are necessary to educate and develop the spirit. I could never have a poor opinion of you, nor have an unkind thought toward you; as you rise, stumble or fall, you only follow the divine law of evolution. I can but wait patiently for you. I shall rush, joyfully, to your assistance, when you need me, if you call upon me for assistance."

"Then it is among the possibilities of the future that I shall not be inclined to seek your companionship as a pleasure, and your help in time of need?"

"It is not only possible, but extremely probable."

There was an accent of truth in this that compelled my conviction. Who was there in the world who really desired continually to live up to his higher self? Was I to consider myself an exception to the whole human race?

My soul continued: "The spirit of cruelty, unkindness and lack of charity for others that prevails in the human race, as it is now developed, arises from the animal nature, which has come up through cruel struggles in the war of evolution. The human race has not yet passed from its sphere of animalism, but it is approaching the border of better things."

"In what way?"

"In the ways that lead men to believe that life does not begin and end with mere materialism; that mere selfish striving is worse than useless, and that only as one approaches to the ideal within himself, can there be any progress in the direction of human advancement."

"Does not religion play any part in the advancement of the race?"

"It is an element, only. It belongs to the childhood of man. It is more often a deterring element. But, what is often called religion, is anything but that. But there is a key-note by which you can always judge."

"What is that?"

"The instant religion departs from its true base of love, it ceases to be religion, and should be discarded. Where it shows one trace of lack of charity, of unkindness, or lack of mercy, it is only a cloak for evil, made more odious by its hypocrisy. When it stoops to cruelty in the name of God, who is the incarnation of love, then there stands forth the most formidable enemy possible to the human race. If the theological caricature of Satan represented anything of real truth, then you can imagine no more perfect type of devil than he, who, in the name of an all-powerful and all-loving God, strikes at his fellow man, because, having different brain formation, or differing association of ideas, he differs from him. But religion, so called, with its varying forms of fetiches, will pass as the period of the animal development of man is passed.

" Will this period be long ? "

" In the movement of the Universe there is no such thing as time. The movement to spiritualize the race has always existed. It is shown in the history of the race. To-day there is an upheaval against materialism, against the dogmas of ancient creeds, and a freedom of opinion that never descends to license. There is growing up an individuality of opinion, a wholesome courage in reaching out into unknown fields, which marks an advance in the slow, upward, never-ending march of a race towards its ultimate destiny of perfection and consequent happiness."

"Am I to be an instrument in the hands of this movement ? "

" If you will ; but its success depends upon no individual. The law of development is absolute. All who wish to be better, to approach more closely to their better selves, are the wise ones of the earth, in that they sooner reach real happiness—and that, every one concedes, is the present object of every living mortal—happiness. But that happiness is only to be found within one's self. All that there is in religion, in mere theory or dogma, can never get beyond this; that perfect happiness lies wholly within the individual himself. He who conquers himself, and rises to his second self, has done all that the law and the prophets could require. It is in this purification and strengthening of the individual that the solution of the problem of a higher civilization alone can be reached. Anything that stimulates the individual to rise to the standard which dwells within himself is to be encouraged. For it is within one's own breast that God alone is to be found. The soul is a part of His essence, and, as such, dwells within the individual, ready, upon the instant, to assist him to rise, and ever patient, forgiving, and always loving, no matter how perverse the spirit, or however persistent the rebellion against the better nature.

" The idea of punishment banishes the one of perfect love. There are delays on the road of progress, by attempts to evade the law, which you might call punishments; but, ultimately, all will arrive at perfect harmony with the divinity that dwells within the most perverse, savage or cruel. Look at human laws, modified as they have been, from time to time, by the advance of the race. When did ever the most cruel punishments act as deterrents to the commission of crime? So long as the cruelty of the animal period continues, you will have cruel laws, such as official murder in revenge for murder committed, and the barbarous methods employed to warp and degrade the unfortunate criminal members of the race, under the plea of protection necessary to be given to society."

I shall never forget the sense of exquisite happiness that permeated my heart, as I sat, during this first interview with my immortal self. Just when the visit ended I do not recall. I faintly remember going to my bedroom in the early morning, where I soon fell asleep. I awoke at ten o'clock, and quickly dressed.

Yes; my soul was right. In the sharp light of the morning, alone, I began to doubt. The experience was a charming one; but was it a reality or a dream? What skillful illusion had not Captain Harcourt been able to weave about me—but with what object?

Well, whether a dream or no, I had certain duties to perform, and no anxiety upon any subject, whether spiritual or material, was going to make me forget that.

CHAPTER XIV.

A NOTEWORTHY SENATORIAL EPISODE, WHICH ENDS IN A CHALLENGE TO A DUEL.

Nothing will better illustrate the overwhelming impression made upon my mind by the incidents of the night in Captain Harcourt's room than the fact that I was made to forget, for the time being, the danger which threatened my friend, Ralph Granger. It did not occur to me, during this first interview with my immortal soul, to ask a single question concerning Ralph; and no thought of guidance or advice suggested itself during this first memorable conversation, which I have reported as faithfully as possible in the last chapter.

Something of this occurred to me the next morning, after breakfast, and I sought Captain Harcourt, before going out. He said to me: "That need not trouble you. The influence of another life, as represented to you last evening, relates, entirely, to your own individuality. If you were to consult your second self upon any subject which occupies you, you would receive no special help or direction. This second and better self prefers to never interfere with the individuality of the person. It is for you to work out your own destiny. Certainly, none of the higher influences of your life could lift for you, if they would, the veil of the future. You, at

present, are involved in a struggle, which is a great
trial to you ; but in the end, it will, doubtless, prove
beneficial. Whether you will be able to save your
friend or not, lies hidden behind the veil, which none
may pierce. It is for you to go ahead and do the best
you can. When you have done all that can be done,
your duty is fulfilled. If you are called upon to suffer,
with your friend, on account of your failure, such is a
part of your destiny, from which you cannot escape."

I must confess that this kind of talk irritated me.
It did not have a practical sound, so I said, abruptly :
"Captain Harcourt, if you will excuse me, I'll not
continue this abstract conversation, but will be off and
at work."

I went straight to the Capitol, as it was now eleven
o'clock. I sought General Starr in his committee
room, where he had only just arrived. "I rather expected you would come," said he, "and destroy the
last possibility of my being able to do any work this
morning. The President sent for me just as I was
leaving the house, and I have been to the White House
again. He takes an altogether different view of the
situation this morning. He is anxious to avoid any
possible scandal, and, if Senator Norton would give
him any kind of an opportunity to yield, he would
change front. He asked me to go to the Senator and
see if some sort of compromise could not be arranged.
For once, his easy-going temperament has triumphed
over his vanity, and he is as anxious to avoid a scandal
as Senator Norton could desire. But what can you do
with impracticable people ? Norton is in one of his

exasperating moods this morning. He has the air of a Julius Cæsar, and will accept nothing but an unconditional backdown on the part of the President. The demands which he has made are impossible to fulfill, and so, between the weaknesses of two vain men, our friend, Granger, will, undoubtedly, suffer. Unless something out of the ordinary way happens, I do not believe that Norton will be thwarted in his purpose to force Granger out of the Cabinet, and I am sure the President is too weak a man to cope, as a politician, with the powerful Senator. If he had any bowels of compassion, or any real breadth of view, he would surrender at once, for the sake of his Cabinet associate."

When I left the General, I went to the gallery of the Senate. There I found the New York papers, which had just arrived. In several of them I saw a mysterious paragraph, hinting at the possibility of a great development in the fight between the President and Senator Norton. To a stranger, these paragraphs meant nothing. To one who was familiar with the situation, their mysterious phrases clearly outlined a threat. Sensational developments were promised. What were these developments, if they did not relate to the misfortune of Secretary Granger?

I entered the correspondents' gallery of the Senate, after reading the papers, and began to watch, carefully, Senator Norton, just as the Senate opened. There were very few people in the galleries at that time. Senator Norton came into his seat, fresh from one of the bath-rooms below the Senate, curled and perfumed by the official barber, radiant with health, physical

superiority and intellectual pride. He fairly swaggered
down the aisle of the Senate chamber, and took his
seat with an aggressive air of insolence, that was particularly noted by certain Southern senators, who sat
near him, and who had been engaged in a sharp political controversy with him the day before. For Senator
Norton was a Northern senator, of an extreme partisan
type. He believed that all the brains and intelligence
of this country, all of the honesty, and all of the real
business ability, were to be found north of Mason and
Dixon's line. In every debate in the Senate, during
the winter of my story, he had gone out of his way to
harass and humiliate the Southern senators. The day
before, he called attention to the fact that upwards of
eighty per cent. of the taxes in this country had been
paid by the North, and that the small percentage of
the tax paid by the South had been through the
Internal Revenue service, or impost upon whiskey and
tobacco. The subject of discussion before the Senate
was one relating to the question of certain expenditures
by the United States Government. It was in this debate that this haughty Northern senator had aggra-
vated his Southern associates to the pitch of madness
by the impertinence and insolence of his criticisms.

The prospect of a repetition of this satirical and
pointed debate filled the galleries soon after the Senate
was formally opened. In the front seat of the private
gallery of the Senate there came a noted lady, who
had filled a great place in the life at Washington. She
was the daughter of a great statesman and the wife of
another—a woman who had been presented at the

various courts of Europe, and whose wealth and position had given her every opportunity for the full enjoyment of high social power. Although forty years of age, she had the figure of a young girl, while only her face showed the traces of the number of years that had passed. She had been given to many flirtations, and her name had been associated questionably with many of the notable men in the brilliant circle of that date. These flirtations had led to much talk, and, ultimately, to an unofficial separation from her husband. Latterly, Senator Norton had become one of her dancing attendants, and, in the light of her flatteries and fascinations, so far forgot himself as to be proclaimed everywhere as her devoted lover. Yet, with the arrogance usual to his character, he pursued the way of this intrigue, without a thonght of any one daring to criticize him, and, perhaps, thinking—so great was his absorption—that no one noticed his actions in this regard.

The relations between the two were almost official in their character, and Mrs. Ray had been so careless upon her side that even easy-going Washington had been forced to cut her acquaintance, and the brilliant dinners and receptions, which knew her once, now saw her only occasionally, and then under protest; had it not been for the still powerful influence of her father, she would have been utterly dropped. As she, languidly, took her seat in the front row of the private gallery, she made a striking picture, in contrast with the prim dames, who are, ordinarily, to be found in this enclosure. She was a pale blonde, who wore, upon this occasion, a dark, jet-beaded bonnet, that stood out in strong contrast against her golden hair. A white, dotted veil, closely drawn, concealed the wrinkles of her face, and made her look young. Her slight figure was clothed in a gray, tailor-made suit, that stood out in sharp contrast against the dark, fur-lined wrap, which fell from her narrow, straight shoulders, as she took her seat. Clapping her lavender-gloved hands, in quite the official manner of the senators below, she summoned a neat page in attendance at the door. He came to her, bowing. She made a request, and, in a moment, he returned with pencil and paper. Then, with an instant comprehension, which Washington has of every incident of this kind, it was made known, through the galleries, that Mrs. Ray was about to write a note to Senator Norton. Senator Norton, himself, turned about in his chair, and looked, in the most ostentatious way, at her, and then she looked back at him, with a sly droop of her gray eyes, which argued an innocence, on her part, hardly in keeping with her character. In the most conspicuous body in the country, where every trivial incident is the subject of gossip, these two people had, apparently, the fatuity to suppose that they were unobserved and uncriticized. In a moment, the note was finished, and then the great Senator, who was then engaged in the fight of his life, arose, with an assumption of carelessness that would not have deceived a child, and backed up, through the middle aisle, to the main entrance of the Senate Chamber. There he stood, with hands behind him, awaiting the secret delivery of a note which everybody had seen written; and, when the little, blonde-headed page came into the door, and actually placed the note within the expectant hand of the statesman, who stood in the easy posture of a man absorbed in very serious thoughts, a smile of amusement ran round the entire galleries. Powerful glasses were brought to bear upon the Senator, and it is more than probable that the contents of the note itself were made known to a number in the gallery, just above his head, as he spread it out, with great impatience, and read it, the moment he returned to his desk.

The incident is worthy of mention only on account of its relation to this story. During the last part of it, Mrs. Granger, accompanied by the Private Secretary of the President of the United States, came into the diplomatic gallery, and took a seat in the front row, next to the iron grille, which separated it from the private gallery, where Mrs. Ray was sitting. The two women were not over a foot apart. Mrs. Granger deliberately turned her shoulder from Mrs. Ray, and, from the look upon the latter's face, it was clear that there was another element to be considered in Senator Norton's fight with the President.

The incident of the note passed around the galleries as a subject of amusing gossip, and, after a time, it reached the diplomatic box, where it was related to the President's private secretary. Ordinarily, the Private Secretary of the President of the United States hears nothing except applications for office. It was such a refreshing change for Colonel Wren, the private secretary in question, that he looked as hilarious as his dignity would permit. He craned his neck over the

gallery, and furtively watched Senator Norton and
Mrs. Ray for some time.   It was evident that he was
seeking to gather in the full bearing of the story for a
report to his master in the White House.   I was sorry
that Mrs. Granger was present, and that she had been
forced to cut Mrs. Ray in so conspicuous a public
place.   I knew that she had enemies enough, without
having the enmity of a vindictive woman, who was, at
that time, so closely allied with Senator Norton, to
increase the adverse influences gathered about her.

A few moments after this, Senator Norton moved to
go into executive session, and the galleries were
cleared.   The motion was made for the purpose of
considering the obnoxious nominations made by the
President.   When the great doors of the Senate
chamber were closed against the public, I was confident that there would be no longer any delay in an
open demonstration of hostility by Senator Norton.

I was particularly impressed by the malignant look
on Mrs. Ray's face, as she rose to leave the gallery.
She glanced, at first, to Senator Norton, to call his
attention, and then back, up to Mrs. Granger, nodding
her head emphatically as she signaled to him. This plain
evidence of her knowledge of the situation was another
one of the singular actions of this noted couple in the
face and eyes of one of the most curious and observing
of publics.

The Senate remained in executive session for several
hours.   The officials who were attendant upon that
body came out from time to time, and their faces were
so colored with excitement, that the outside corps of

newspaper watchers became convinced that something very unusual was going on inside. The executive sessions of the Senate are secret only in name. In these sessions, nominations and treaties are considered. These secret sessions are rigidly adhered to by the exclusive Senate, although, so far as the public is concerned, their transactions might as well be conducted in open day. The senators are, practically, on their honor, not to tell what occurs during these sessions ; but no method has ever been discovered for making more than fourscore men keep secrets, and so full details . of everything leaks out, in some irregular way, within the shortest possible time after each session is closed.

The Senate doors were closed until late that afternoon. I returned up-town before the adjournment took place, and it was not until later that evening that I learned the occasion of the extraordinary prolongation of the secret session.

That evening I had been invited to dine at General Starr's. The guests were largely official, and we went into the dining-room about half-past seven. Mrs. Granger was among the guests, and I was seated not far from her in the order of the arrangement of the table. It was her last public appearance in Washington society. Mrs. Starr was obliged to excuse the absence of her husband from the dinner-table. He had not yet returned from the Senate. There were two other empty chairs at this table—those of other senatorial guests. About nine o'clock, the three missing senators came in. They were inflamed with excitement, and pallid from fatigue. The prolonged session of the

Senate had been the subject of a great deal of gossip at the dinner-table; but, when the senators arrived, no one thought to question them until the preceding courses of the dinner had been served to them, and enough had been drank to restore them to the normal condition of comfort, when gossip begins, and flows on like an unending stream.

There was no sensational recital of what had occurred, but, by piecemeal, it came out, through chance remarks of the various senators to those immediately about them, that Senator Norton had been most conspicuous in the debate upon the appointments in question, and had made a perfectly furious attack upon the President. In his talk, he had been so careless as to again stir up the Southern senators, who had not yet gotten over their quarrel of the day preceding. One Southern senator in question, a former General in the Confederate service, had dared to stand up for the President, although not in political sympathy with him. Senator Norton had turned upon him with lightning-like fury, openly calling him a "toady," and directly accusing him of having made a bargain with the President, exchanging his services for some dirty, little office. This brought the Southern General to the front. With eyes flashing fire, and a voice trembling with emotion, and hoarse with rage, he went to the extreme of insult by calling Senator Norton a liar. There were no doubtful phrases used in the conversation that ensued. The plainness of speaking led to violent protests on both sides of the Chamber from senators who were anxious to save the dignity of that body above all things. The

Southern senator was so wild and uncontrollable that his friends could not help his challenging Senator Norton to mortal combat.

It sounds very childish ; but the discussion which followed related entirely to this challenge. The Southern General insisted that it was the only way to curb the insolence of such a man as Senator Norton. He doubted whether Senator Norton would care to go out against him ; but he felt his duty, as a Southern gentleman, was to send the challenge, and he notified Senator Norton, at the close of their controversy, that he would hear from him again.

The strangest part of the story was that Senator Norton was resolved to accept the challenge, and fight the duel, if necessary. A committee of senators was appointed to adjust the difficulty, and, for the first time in the history of that body, this august assemblage was obliged to officially recognize the fact of the duel, and appoint a committee to settle the question of personal insult, according to the principles of the code of honor.

It was not until the ladies had retired from the table that we got the full particulars. The ex-Confederate General, who challenged Senator Norton, had made use of certain expressions, in the heat of his anger, which plainly pointed to the relations then existing between Senator Norton and Mrs. Ray. It was brought out by a question of personal loyalty, where the Southern General more than intimated that the Senator had better raise any other question than one of personal loyalty of character. He made a direct

reference to this intrigue, which had been so conspicuously made prominent in the open sessions of the
Senate that day.   It was this allusion which provoked
Senator Norton to such a condition that he was willing
to accept the challenge.

It was in the quiet talk after dinner that General
Starr, sarcastically, reviewed the situation.   "We are
supposed to be statesmen," said he, "and there is a
current impression throughout the country that we are
here for the purpose of serving the public ; yet, I have
never known a time in the history of the Senate when
there was so much silly, boyish quarreling about nothing, and such an absolute forgetting of all of our real
duties.   Take Norton; if his worst enemy was at
present directing him, he could not lead him into more
open traps.   He is a man of great ability, and of high
character, as men go.   He is incapable of making a
dishonest penny, and no one could improperly influence
his vote in any direction, and, yet, here he is, running
the road to ruin as fast as any man can go.   He began
this fight, with the President, with some basis of political reason ; but he has carried it to such an extreme
that he cannot hope for public approval.   When a man
is going to engage in such a fight as that, he should, at
least, observe prudence in regard to his private conduct.   After compromising himself openly, in a personal
way, he has not had strength of mind enough to refuse
this challenge, which, of course, can only result in
ridicule.   The day of dueling in Washington has
passed.   Why," said the General, "it was only the
other day that I, myself, had the honor of receiving a

challenge. It came from a Georgia member of the House, who objected to something that I said in an open debate in the Senate. He actually sent two of his friends to me. They came to me on the Senate floor, and presented the challenge. I read it through, and, then, tore it in two, in their faces, and cast it in the waste basket. They asked if that was my answer, and I said: 'My dear swashbuckler friends, I have not lived to my time of life for nothing. I do not propose to make a fool of myself now. If you think it is a question of courage, why, let it go at that. Stay; I will send a message back. Tell your friend who sent the challenge that, if he dares to take up the subject with me personally, I will give him the biggest threshing he ever had in his life,' and this," added the General, "was the end of the proposed duel."

When we entered the drawing-room, I found Mrs. Granger still among the guests. She never looked more radiantly beautiful than then. She sat in an easy chair, under the full, blazing light of huge chandeliers. Her evening dress, which followed closely the lines of her beautiful figure, was black lace, accentuated by bits of orange color, in the form of knots of ribbon, and a line here and there of very narrow, delicate embroidery. Her blue-black hair, combed up high from her forehead, was carried back in a Grecian knot. A diamond star gleamed in the dark mass, the single ornament of her royally-posed head. The fatigue and excitement of the last few days gave a delicate tint of pallor to her dark-olive face. Her eyes were unusually dark and brilliant. No one, who did not know her well, would have thought that there was anything in the world that could annoy or disturb her. As I came up, several members of the diplomatic colony stood about in attitudes of polite admiration. As I entered the room, she summoned me to her by a quiet glance, and then, by some mysterious process, those about her were dismissed, without their apparently knowing it, and we were left, for the moment, alone.

Waving, calmly, to and fro, a brilliantly scarlet fan, she said in even-measured tones : "I am much obliged to you for what you have done, but you will not succeed in saving me. Just before I left the house this evening, my husband received a sealed package from a messenger, who came into the library as I was bidding him good-bye for the evening. He was obliged to excuse himself from coming to this dinner, for the President sent word during the latter part of the afternoon that he wished to see him during that evening on a matter of great importance. I know, from the look upon his face, after he had opened the package, and read the first letter that some one had sent to him, for his private perusal, the story which Senator Norton showed to you. As he glanced at the first letter, he thrust the whole package into his desk and locked it. He then turned to me, and said that I would have to excuse him, as he was going to the White House, and was already behind time. From his manner, I did not infer that he really grasped the case in its relations to me. As I came out of the house to come here, I saw Mrs. Ray seated in a hansom cab upon the opposite corner, paying the very messenger, who had just left my husband's library. So I conclude that all that Senator Norton knew, she knew, and that that information is now in my husband's hands, and that I go from here to an explanation which, probably, will result disastrously."

I could not control myself as she did. It is only women who can do that, carry a calm face over a tortured heart in the face of the enemy, the public. I made some involuntary expression of sympathy, when she checked me, with a glance, as she continued: "I think, on the whole, I am relieved. The suspense, at least, is over. I have felt confident, all the time, that this would come to my husband's knowledge, and that life, hereafter, as I have lived it, would be impossible. I have firmly resolved to admit everything, and to have no further deception. This I do with the full knowledge that my husband will not forgive me, and that the sin which I have committed, although not one of deliberate planning, is one which he will regard as the greatest of all, in that it affects his financial honor."

With this, she arose with gentle courtesy, and bade farewell to her hostess, and the group of friends about her. I walked out with her to her carriage, and saluted her, with tears in my eyes, as she sank back with a short sigh and said to the coachman: "Drive home." There was an unintentional pathos in the accent and expression in her pronunciation of the word "home," which moved me deeply. This woman had committed a serious fault, but she went forward to meet its consequences with a courage which, in my judgment, more than offset the error committed.

CHAPTER XV.

PICTURES OF THE SCENES IN THE GRANGER HOUSE-HOLD TRAGEDY.

I hurried straight back to the hotel, and sought out Captain Harcourt's room. I found him, as before, seated, looking off and out at what he called pictures painted for him by his immortal soul.

It was midnight when I entered the room. I found again the Oriental setting of the chamber of the night before, and this sight thrilled me with the hope that I might once more meet, in the hour of this dire emergency, my second self, and from him obtain, perhaps, a suggestion of something to be done. It was the first time during the day that I had really thought of him, or had had any real desire to see him.

Scarcely had I seated myself, when Captain Harcourt said: "You have returned at an earlier hour than I expected you. Do you care again to meet your second self? Because you must, first, have the wish, and, second, you would be helpless in your desire to see, if you did not have, for the first few times, the aid of some one initiated in these mysteries."

I gave him my hand, and I noted that the Captain's hand, as it returned the pressure, gave me a sensation of wholesome strength. His hand marked the maximum of electrical conditions, by being dry, warm, throbbing through every vein with an exquisite vitality.

The next moment, the blue clouds hovered between us, and then, as they cleared, I saw that a third individuality, that of my soul, had again joined us. He was seated opposite me, with the same tranquil expression on his face, and the same look of kindness he had the night before. "You see," said I, "I really did want to see you again."

"Yes; your desire is not wholly unexpected. I said that it was possible, and even probable, that you should not care to see me again, but in time of trouble, when all ordinary resources fail one, people sometimes turn to extraordinary means. You started out this morning, confident that you could do something. To-night you have come to me, and so acknowledge your defeat."

"Yes; it is true, I have done all that I can, and I see nothing, now, but failure for all my efforts. Can you help me?"

"I do not possess any power that you do not have. I am of you. If I have powers of seeing more clearly than you do, and of judging more correctly, that is only where I would surpass you in an effort to right such a grievous wrong as the one you have had in your mind during the last two days; but what is taking place now is in accordance with law. The family which you know, is broken up, and their happiness, as generally understood, destroyed; but, yet, the after-results will be good. Each has to learn his lesson in the world. The character of your friend, Mr. Granger, is

that of a just man—but justice as construed and understood by the world at large. He is what the world
would call a perfectly just man; and, being that, he is
a perfectly merciless one. Such justice your friend,
Granger, has shown to his wife. What the world will
be pleased to call a tragedy, has already taken place in
their house."

"What do you mean?" said I.

"Would you like me to describe the scene that took
place in that household, upon Mrs. Granger's return?
For you know that the eyes of the soul pierce through
material things, and I have seen every detail of that
story, which will seem so sad to you, from the first to
the conclusion."

"The conclusion?"

"Yes; the conclusion; but it would be better, perhaps,
for me to give you that story, as it occurred, in a series
of pictures. You shall be given, for the time, my eyes,
and you shall see as I have seen, and you shall hear as
I have heard, the conclusion of this chapter."

The great walls of the room opposite now disappeared. There was a sound of murmuring music, a
shifting, gray, cloud mass fell for a moment, and then
the curtain rose, disclosing, like a set scene upon the
stage, the interior of the library of the Granger household. It was a room with which I was thoroughly
familiar. I saw, again, its long line of books, its easy
chairs, its dark rugs and polished floor, dimly lighted
by a swinging light, which hung over a great central
desk, in front of which sat, pale, stern and waiting,
Secretary Ralph Granger. I hardly recognized my

friend. His look of confident, cheerful serenity was gone; it had given way to the severe, grave lines of a judge, waiting for a prisoner, charged with high crime, about to be brought before him. He had just returned from his conference with the President, and had learned from the latter of the threatened line of attack of Senator Norton. He had learned, only, from the President that Senator Norton proposed to drive him out of the Cabinet, but the means to be employed were not then disclosed to him. Confident in his own honor and integrity, he had returned home about eleven o'clock, and had sought the refuge of his library; when there, he remembered the package that was brought to him early in the evening. It now flashed upon him that the solution of the mystery might be found in this package. He had just finished reading its contents, when the scene in his chamber was laid open to my eyes. I saw him rise and pace the floor like one distraught, and then, remembering the necessity for control, saw him call a servant, and heard him say to him: "Tell Mrs. Granger, the moment she comes in, to kindly come to the library, as I have something of importance to say to her." Involuntarily, I trembled at the deliberate accent of this calm order. I remembered, my friend was never so deeply wrought as when he appeared to be the most quiet and self-contained. In ordinary intercourse, he was expansive and buoyant. A reserved manner, and a low, even tone, indicated, always, with him suppressed excitement. After the order was given, there followed a few moments of silence, during which Mr. Granger returned to the packet and its contents, which were all spread out in the glare of the central light.

It was a curious sensation to sit, watching the pro-gress of events which had already occurred. The reconstitution of the scene of the Granger household made much more of an impression on my mind, for the moment, through the possibilities of its being done, rather than by the incidents themselves as they were presented. But this was only for a moment. Suddenly, I heard the sharp click of horses' hoofs on the smooth asphalt pavement, then the opening of a carriage door, the ring of a bell, the opening of the heavy front door, the casual directions to the servant; then my heart throbbed with pity as, with my sharpened sense, I heard the soft footfalls of Mrs. Granger, going straight down through the hall to the library, where her husband was waiting for her.

The scene in the library now became even more sharply accentuated. I could see every line in Gran-ger's face. With an impulsive man there might have been the cry of anger at the sight of his wife, who came in easy, calm, and apparently indifferent, as if scandal and intrigue were far away from her serene, calm countenance.

Yet, there was a look on her face which showed that she knew. But Mr. Granger, in his perfect justice, met her with more than usual courtesy. He said: "If you are not too tired, I should like to talk with you about a subject which has been brought to my attention this evening, and which, to all appearances, should interest you personally."

Mrs. Granger sank down in the chair opposite the desk from her husband, and supporting herself on one elbow on the desk, she half turned to him, with an air of polite inquiry. As she thus turned, the rich, dark, furred cloak slipped down from her ivory-tinted shoulders, leaving the delicate lines of her figure in clear relief against this warm, rich background. While her husband gathered up the papers in front of him, she, with great deliberation, unbuttoned and removed the long, white gloves which had reached nearly to the shoulders; her drooping head, the line of the neck, the curve of the shoulders, the gleam of the left arm, lying bare upon the desk, while its mate was hidden in the fur of the falling cloak, made a picture which might have caused the mind of the most upright and just man to waver from too severe a judgment.

There was a hopeless resignation in the attitude, and at the same time, a quiet resolution, which should have warned the judge, who sat opposite, that, in trying a case, leniency is sometimes the only real justice.

Secretary Granger now took up the papers, with the precision of a lawyer in court, as he said: " I propose to call to your attention certain alleged facts which were sent to me this evening in the packet you see before me. It is but fair to add that this came to me from an anonymous source, and did it not contain documents, signed by responsible people, I should not condescend to trouble you with it. Allow me to recapitulate what is charged." After summarizing, in a very precise manner, Senator Norton's story, Mr. Granger said: " It appears to be undisputed that certain appointments in my department were given to certain men, and that certain contracts followed those appointments. It was with my own hand that those appointments and contracts were made and awarded. It is charged that they were paid for, and that the proceeds of such alleged payments can be directly traced to me. In other words—that I am a dishonest man, who has forfeited all claim to honor, and have committed a crime for which I can be impeached, and disfranchised as a citizen."

I could see Mrs. Granger turn white, and then I heard her say: "What is the evidence, Ralph, against you personally?"

"We have here," said he, "a payment of a large sum of money to one of your relatives, and we have, further, several foolish letters from him, in which he plainly indicates that a part of that money was paid to some member of this household. If it was not paid to me, then it was either paid to my son"—(at this the mother shrank)—"to one of my daughters, or"—pausing deliberately—"to their gracious mother, who, carries my honor in her hands." There was a spasm of pain which contracted the features of Mrs. Granger. She bowed her head to the head to which she had never humbly bowed before, as she said, in notes barely above a whisper: "It is I—I—alone who am guilty." Then a look came over her husband's face, which made her shrink as if from a blow. Then she put up her hand, seeking feebly to shield herself from his stern, cruel glance. "No," said he in reply, "I will not forgive you; neither do I propose to make any extravagant scene. You have failed in your duty; you have proved yourself to be an unworthy woman; you have done all that lies within your power to ruin and disgrace an honored name, and to leave a legacy of shame to your children. The world shall never know what I think of you. I am ready now to take that shame upon my own shoulders. So far as the public is concerned, I shall be the guilty one. I know enough of your nature to understand and appreciate you. I feel sure that it is a fault that could never be repeated; but life for us, as we knew it, is ended. I will protect you always with my name; but in reality our union is broken, and we stand divorced and separated from the moment that you confessed your guilt."

The severity of his sentiments left Mrs. Granger crushed. She made no attempt to speak one word of defence. After a few moments of painful silence she arose, and gathering her cloak about her, she moved out of the library and up the stairs to her room. I saw her enter that room, close it afterwards, and then, pausing with her hand over her heart, under the dim light of a tiny electric lamp, she swayed to and fro, seeking vainly to control herself, and to fight against the furious fit of sobbing, the deep, passionate gasps of which reached to the inner citadel of her life. She took an uncertain step forward, then, all at once, stumbled, her head striking against the chimney-piece, causing a cruel blow above the temple, and then the poor woman fell flat upon her face, lying in the empty grate, with her beautiful face buried in its dead ashes, while her evening robe and prostrate figure made a mass of dark colors upon the white wolf-skin robe, which lay in front of what had been her favorite lounging place in this white and gold sitting-room of her favorite fancy.

As I looked upon this piteous spectacle, I saw rise, above the dark figure, a blue ball of light. This ball shone first with a soft glimmer, and then the light became more intense, and out of that light I saw, gradually, grow and expand the face of Mrs. Granger, still wearing the expression of pain and horror; while nearer, bending over her in a protecting way, with outstretched arms, stood Mrs. Granger perfected—her immortal soul waiting to take in hand the spirit that had just escaped, and to accompany it to the beginning of some other existence, where a compensation for the seeming misfortune of the one just passed might be found.

CHAPTER XVI.

A STUDY OF SOME OF THE CONDITIONS OF HUMAN ADVANCEMENT.

For me, the death of Mrs. Granger was the end of the intrigue, so far as my personal interest was concerned. Her sudden death caused a great sensation. It was attributed to heart-failure, and many were the moralizing editorials written upon the cruel exigencies of high social life in Washington. Ralph Granger resigned from the Cabinet, within the hour, after finding his wife's body. He returned to his Western home after the funeral, taking his children with him. He had a long and free talk with the President before going, in which he disclosed the story of the intrigue, as it had been revealed to him. The President asked him to stay; but, in his heart, he was glad to have him go, now that the possibility of an open scandal had become so great. I had frequent conferences, in these days, with Granger, but he never took me into his confidence. He never knew the part I had tried to play in protecting him, and this was just as well; if he had known, he could not have had me so near him when he was winding up his Washington affairs, as he shrank from coming in contact with any one whom he remotely suspected of having a knowledge of the Norton story.

Too much had become known for him to entirely escape. One or two publications hinted that Mrs. Granger's death was a suicide, and others vaguely surmised a scandal, hidden by Granger's resignation. But Washington is fickle-minded, and the incident of the senatorial duel overshadowed all else. Then there came the grave settlement of the duel by an august committee of senatorial grandfathers, and, at last, Washington was given a chance to laugh, and to say, gently, malicious things—an opportunity which it never neglects. After a brief season of chaffing, Senator Norton was stricken down by an illness of so dangerous and serious a character as to eliminate him, for some time, as a political factor, and so the easy-going President was, once more, contented, and more and more convinced that Providence was a special friend of his, who looked out, at the proper time, for the discomfiture of his enemies, and for the removal of all disagreeable obstacles from his path. There grew up in his mind the sincere conviction that destiny had marked him for a very happy fate, and he began to plan for his renomination with a cheerful confidence.

The moment Ralph Granger had departed, I resumed my customary routine of life. I felt dull and disappointed. I was unhappy over my failure to stem, in the slightest degree, the onward march of a particular fate, whose advancing shadow I had so clearly seen.

But, when I was with Captain Harcourt, the disappointment was gone, and, then, some way, I was made to feel that everything that occurred was in accordance with an inevitable law, and, whether called fate or something else, each mortal had to pass through so many stages of experience before he could earn the right to immortality and perfect happiness.

Faintly, I began to have an understanding of the wisdom of the divine law that kept one's memory dark as to the past. How could one find the strength to bear the burdens of one existence, if the memory had, chained to it, the endless memories of long previous ones? How hideous would then be the future, stretching out, without apparent end of seemingly useless struggling.

Something of this I said to Captain Harcourt, a few nights after Mrs. Granger's death.

To it he replied: "The remedy for all this lies in the cultivation of the better self. In this, the nation resembles the individual. There is a soul to a nation— its ideal—and this ideal is only reached by the units which compose it rising to the high standard planted within by the overruling Deity."

So, gently, and through the aid of his kind companionship, I was led, more and more, to woo the intimacy of my immortal self. The first pleasure of a gratified curiosity in talking with him was succeeded by a sensation of uneasiness. I do not believe there are many people who could, easily and quickly, become at ease in the constant company of one who was constantly a measure of perfection for every act and thought.

But I soon found comfort in a plan that Captain Harcourt submitted to me, from the Island of Nolos. He said to me, one evening, after I had come in from a busy and profitless day: "I shall soon be obliged to leave Washington, and, before going, I wish to outline to you the work that Doctor Longman gave me to do before coming here. I want you to take up this work, as a member of our society, for the improvement of the world. Your character has undergone, recently, a sharp change, and your disposition is, I am sure, more in accordance with our needs. Your experience here, as an observer and writer, has trained you for our work; but all would have been useless, had not your disposition been made over by the ardent fire of a recent bit of unselfishness. Now you are in the mood and condition to be of use, while, if the opportunity should pass, you might again become indifferent, and go drifting once more. Now, honestly tell me what has been the result of the last ten years of your work as a writer at Washington?"

"Not much, I can assure you."

"What has been, most frequently, the subject of your correspondence during the last ten years?"

"Current news."

"What has been the standard of news at Washington?"

"The leading events of the political day."

"What have been considered leading events?"

"Personal scandals have always ranked first. Political intrigues of all sorts—anything detrimental to the character of any prominent public man—have always been considered desirable."

"Do you recall ever attempting to create a sensation

by publishing an exposure of all the good deeds of a public man ?"

"Oh, never ! "

"The evil predominating in the news reports of the day is only a reflection of the time. It is a corollary of the selfish strivings of all. Who comes to Washington to serve any one but himself, from the President down? All may start with the highest motives; but, in the war, here, for supremacy, selfishness so rules, that he who would live in all this contention of malicious striving must learn to strike and bite at every one who stands in his way."

"How can this be remedied ?"

"It can be done only through years of toil; yet, the beginning can be made through the presentation of ideal conditions, in contrast with conditions that no one would claim are just or correct."

"But, how can this be done?"

"It goes back to the system of the Island of Nolos. Remember, the power that comes from there gives an adept the power to see things as they are, and to see them as they really should be. I have the power to show you this in such clear pictures, that they will have, to you, the emphasis of actuality. With the aid of your own immortal soul, I will reveal to you the real soul of this national life, and you shall make a permanent record of your impressions. This shall be the first part of the work assigned to you. Do you accept the task?"

"Gladly."

"Then I want you, first, to go over, with me, some of

the results of Doctor Longman's observations upon the human race, as it has, thus far, been developed. He who taught me ever dwelt upon the innate goodness of the human type. You must start out with a profound belief in the real goodness of every one. It may be encrusted with ignorance, surface cruelty and ironclad habits of indifference; but, in each man dwells a soul, a part of the divinity which has shaped all creation, and, when you have that fact once in your mind, it will not be possible for you to despise or hate any one. You can but feel sorry for the unfortunate individual whose education and surroundings have closed his eyes in ignorance, or else have turned all his energies in the wrong direction. For, I repeat, as the proof of the assertion of the innate goodness of every one is to be found in the fact that the only real happiness ever found in this world is the result of some act of kindness or unselfishness, that is in accordance with this higher nature. The reason why there is so much misery and unhappiness in this world is owing to the antagonism to the underlying principle of the doctrine of loving kindness. Those who live brightest in history, and have the warmest corners in our hearts, are those who have taught the doctrine of unselfishness, and have lived for others. The one name in history that overshadows all others is the Christ man. Why does he surpass in name, in glory, in reverence, all others? Because we all believe in his divinity, and his kinship to God? No; because, in the same sense, we are all divine, and equally children of the Creator. It is because his life was, throughout, a sacrifice for others, a life of love and thought for his fellow man, his living up to the divinity of the immortal soul possessed by every one, and his death, as the culmination of a life of purity, self-denial and sacrifice. If it were not for our possession of the same divinity, do you suppose that his life would have left the same impression upon the succeeding ages, in spite of the mockery of his principles by the churches built up in his name? If the people of this world could only be brought to adopt his standard of loving kindness towards their fellow creatures, poverty, misery and crime would soon be made to disappear."

I will not go any further in this chapter, but will, I think, better illustrate his meaning by giving as careful a description as possible of the pictures he presented me of the ideal nation, and the possibilities of our future development in something less, it is to be hoped, than the one hundred million years required to perfect a planet.

CHAPTER XVII.

PICTURING IDEAL POSSIBILITIES OF OUR FUTURE NATIONAL LIFE.

Out of the many pictures presented, I remember none that impressed me more, as a whole, than the one given to me of the National Capitol.

It was upon the first evening of the beginning of my work of study as an adept of the religion of the Island of Nolos. The pictures came as we talked. My soul sat near me. Sometimes the explanation came from him, sometimes from Captain Harcourt. I gathered, at the outset, that the ideal Capital of the nation was one that should present an absolute standard of perfection for the nation at large. The ideal must be reached at the center of national existence before the work of the uplifting of a nation should be reached. But, to the pictures.

First, in the ideal picture, the Capitol, as it should be, was viewed by me from the standpoint of Capitol Hill. Here I was overwhelmed with admiration at the magnificent proportions of this legislative temple. All of the crudities of the central building, now so out of harmony with the wings, were gone. The building was in the form of a Greek cross, each wing a pure and harmonious complement of the other. Below the central building stretched away terraces, adorned, here and there, with statuary, representing beauty in every form of correct line, and groups, commemorative of the nation's history, the handiwork of great artists, who had mastered their art through the knowledge given them by their diviner selves. As I looked at the Capitol building, I saw, revealed through its white marble walls, which were pierced by my vision, the noble adornments of pictures, statues, and decorations, conceived in the highest possibility of art. Here the full limit of harmony, color and form had been reached. The problems of light and ventilation had been solved, so that the sweetness of the air and the purity of the light were borne in upon me, in strong contrast with my memory of the hideous foulness and diginess of the atmosphere of the great Capitol building, as it now exists.

The legislative chambers were alike in the high character of adornment. The white marble and gold of the walls, the carved ivory of the benches—for desks had been abolished—gave an atmosphere of great purity to halls where only questions of benefit to the public could be considered. With such surroundings of harmony and simplicity, the minds of the legislators were influenced corresponding to the elevated character of their work.

In explanation of this extreme attention shown in every detail to the laws of beauty, my soul said : " In time, men will come to learn that there is nothing so influential in lifting up men as the cultivation of beauty. They will find that, throughout nature, beauty is the universal law ; and the nearer they approach to beauty in their surroundings, the more rapid their advance to a higher civilization. It will be found that it costs no more to have things made in beautiful forms than in ugly ones. With such surroundings, the mind becomes more impressible to the teachings of the higher life. Architecture, sculpture and painting have done more to raise up men than generations of moral discourse."

Leaving the interior of the great home of legislative government, I passed, quickly, to the southern terrace, and took a quick, comprehensive look at the great city that stretched out at my feet. I was anxious to get, first, a superficial view of everything, and not seek to look into the actual working of an ideal government until I had become more familiar with its outward face.

The scene below was lighted by the bright, warm sun and clear atmosphere of an early May. Pennsylvania Avenue, lined by noble trees, was flanked upon either side by grand piles, representing the various great offices of the government. Upon the left, the beautiful edifices were surrounded by parks, representing the highest art of the landscape-gardener. Stretched away, along drives and graded walks, to the silvery Potomac—over which were numerous memorial bridges, covered with statues and memorial tablets, in memory of those who had done the most to prove themselves worthy of honor at the hands of the Republic—upon the heights of the Virginia shore, was a line of temples, bearing such inscriptions as to clearly show their character; for, as I looked long at any particular portion of the picture, it suddenly grew upon my vision, until every detail stood out distinctly, as if I were close upon it. Here were universities, schools, temples for public ceremonials, and the many buildings required for the teaching of a perfected civilization. Each art and science had its home, with outlying buildings flanking it, wherein were stored every attainable object for the elucidation of the subject to be treated.

Upon the heights, to the northwest of Washington, was a series of State buildings; for each State had built a palace for the housing of its senators and representatives. These palaces were vast, and gave to each more room than could be found in any modern house. Each foreign nation had selected some goodly site for the home of its ambassador. The variety of architecture was great, but a spirit of harmony ran through the whole.

Upon the heights at the right, at the head of what is now Sixteenth Street, was the palace of the President of the United States, overtopping all of the edifices of the city in its graceful lines and richness of adornment. To its right and left were the palaces of the Cabinet ministers, and other universities, museums, and palaces of the arts.

The prevailing color was a soft, yellow-white. Upon examination of the material, I found it to be a composition, which hardened greatly under exposure, having the solidity and richness of marble, without its coldness.

The streets, clean, paved and swept, were adorned

with numerous parks, and were always flanked by
double rows of trees.   The vehicles flying about were
light, and, being propelled by electricity, moved swiftly
and noiselessly, leaving no dirt, and needing no special
track for their guidance.

There was not a poor or ugly-looking house in the
city.   Even the smallest were perfect in their lines of
beauty and in their adornment.   To the south, as far
as the eye could reach, stretched away the houses of
the humbler class, but all were of the character in
which the rich men of to-day would be proud to dwell.

Coming closer to the life in the streets, I observed
that all wore happy and contented faces.   Their dress
and their beauty suggested the princes of the fairy
tales of my childhood.   I searched everywhere for an
ugly face.   " Has perfection, then, been reached by
this race ? " I asked.

" No," was the reply of my soul ; " the people you see
have arrived at the utmost of their possibilities in this
world ; but I have shown you the Capital at a period
when it has reached its ideal in company with some of
the leading centers of the world ; but the same ideal
condition will not be reached by the entire world until
some centuries later.   These people, here, send out an
influence, which has now become overwhelming ; for, in
this picture, you will see that the world, in all that directs
and controls its most important acts, has reached a plane,
where good, instead of evil, predominates.   The people
you see here are the products of centuries of happy,
beauty-seeking lives.   Naturally, they have taken on
more and more, with each generation, the form of their

higher selves, until the beauty of the individual has reached a point where it is in harmony with the surroundings of this higher civilization. You will never see an unkind expression, nor meet with a discourteous word in this community, where the highest pleasure found is in making others happy."

As I looked, I became so interested in the life of this ideal city, with its temples and shining beauties of an earthly paradise, that I became curious to study the details of what appeared to be the perfection of human government.

CHAPTER XVIII.

THE LIFE OF THE NATION AFTER IDEAL CONDITIONS ARE REACHED.

One of the most interesting pictures shown described the preparation necessary for holding a public place in an ideal State. It came, gradually, to the consciousness of the people, that the science of human government, being the most complicated, and the one requiring the greatest study, it was of the utmost importance that men should be trained properly for filling public positions, and that no man should be elected to any high office who had not learned the requirements of the position, and who was not possessed of the education which would justify his selection. When men were properly qualified and elected, they were permitted, when faithful, by a very just sentiment, to hold office for life. It was felt that it was very unjust to detach men from their private pursuits for the purpose of serving the public, and then send them back again, after a few years of faithful service, for no other reason than the giving an opportunity to new men. Politics thus had become a noble profession, to which the best brains and minds of the country were directed.

Schools were established throughout the country for the training of men who intended to seek public office, and no one was permitted to hold even the humblest place who had not passed through some one of these schools. Congress, as I knew it, was an assemblage of men, brought together by haphazard from various sections of the country; some of them very ignorant, and some of them very astute and skillful. The ignorant new-comer often learned what was to be done only on the eve of his retirement. The rotation in office, which existed at the writing of this story, had had a most baleful effect upon our politics. Very few good men could afford to sacrifice the most important period of their life to the doubtful experiment of obtaining a success in the uncertain field of politics. In the ideal state, the schools taught all the correct theories of politics. They proceeded upon the theory that the experience of nations, through centuries of study, counted for something, and that, for a man to start *de novo*, and to attempt to establish, for himself, an original line of study, or theory, concerning politics, was absurd, and a wretched waste of time. Certain principles relating to politics have been accepted by all the nations of the world, and, to go against the established facts of the past, was considered foolish. One of the most important schools was the school of finance, for in nothing had the statesmen of the past had such wide differences. In this school, the ground principles were taught, that no system of finance could be considered sound which was against the general practice of civilized nations, and that, however correct the theory might be, it was wholly impracticable, unless it was generally accepted. It was

further taught that no nation could afford, in its financial policy, to make exceptions, for itself, to the general
practice of nations, without incurring great loss. This
same principle was extended to the teachings of other
economic questions. While free trade had been recognized as correct in the abstract theory, it was a question
which required the united action of nations to produce
harmonious and successful results. In other words,
that free trade was not possible without the united
action of all the civilized nations of the world.

One of the interesting features of the education
of public men was the provision for their visiting
other countries. Every year, a certain number of the
candidates, who had, by their diligence, and by the
display of ability, acquired the right, were sent to
foreign countries for two or three years of study and
travel. Those who aspired to hold a high place in the
National council began their career, after graduating
from the schools, in the employment of the municipality.
Municipal affairs had long been divorced from National
and State politics. Cities were governed exactly as if
they were corporations, and only the stockholders were
allowed to have anything to say about the way the
city should be managed. In other words, it was the
property-owners, alone, who had the right, in affairs
purely municipal, to say what should be done. These
property-owners elected, from time to time, boards of
directors, who, being themselves interested in the
actual property of the community, planned all expenditures upon the most economical lines. Every expenditure was made openly, so that the public had an oppor-

tunity of scrutinizing, daily, the expenditures and acts
of the Central Board of Directors. The result of this
was that there was no waste, no money misappropriated
to improper purposes. The municipalities eliminated
every poor building from the town, and built up a
system of high-class tenements for the use of the poor
people, who were enabled to have absolutely comfortable and healthful quarters at half the rent they
were paying now, while the city received, from these
rents, a clear five per cent. on the investment. There
being no money wasted in corruption funds, every
dollar which was collected was honestly and economi-
cally expended; so that the various cities of the Union
gradually turned their attention to public improvements, which were not possible under the wasteful and
ignorant mismanagement of the past. Streets were
now perfectly paved and lighted. The architecture of
all the great buildings controlled by the municipality
was in accordance with the most perfect lines, while
schools, throughout the community, were established
to teach the mechanical arts.

Attendance upon these schools was compulsory for
children of the class who were too poor to pay taxes.
The municipal government saw to it that every child
of the poorer classes in the town was educated, given
a fine, physical training, and, when absolutely necessary,
he was fed at the expense of the town. It was found,
after a long experience, that this system did not en-
courage pauperism, and that the moneys thus expended
did not equal, at any time, the amounts now spent
every year for the protection of society against the

criminal classes, which come from uneducated, un-
trained, and neglected classes of society.

In each town there was a great forum. It was the
most beautiful place in the municipality. About it
were grouped temples and palaces devoted to public
uses. Every art and science received the encouragement of the municipality. Every student who displayed the slightest talent was encouraged and stimulated to put forth every effort for the full development of his genius. Amusements were provided for
the public by the municipality. Every public building
was open night and day, so that no one was so
poor but what he could find a warm, well-lighted and
sheltered place, whenever he should choose to seek it.
Every district of the town was provided with skilled
musicians, who played, every day, in some of the
halls, whenever the weather was bad ; and, when it
was good, in the parks. The children who did well in
the industrial school were promoted to the higher
schools, where the arts were taught by accomplished
masters. The person who was considered most important in the community was he who could, by his
genius, contribute in the highest degree to the stock of
beauty of the community, whether in the form of
architecture, sculpture or painting. The artists were
among those of the first rank, standing equal even to
the public men, who devoted their entire lives to serving the public, and to forgetting self. Public baths
were constructed by the municipality in every form
—large and small—so that every district, however
crowded, or however select, had, at its disposal, lux-

urious bathing-places, made free by the municipality
to every one who wished to come. More than this—
light and heat were furnished by the municipality. In
the perfection of mechanical appliances, it was found
that Mr. Keeley, the Philadelphia inventor, had laid
the way for this; so that the furnishing of light and
heat, free, really meant nothing, so far as actual expenditures were concerned. The force discovered by Mr.
Keeley, which was the underlying principle of electricity, was utilized, by this time, to such an extent,
that light and heat were taken from the ether of the
Universe, and distributed in such a way that every
home was brilliantly heated and warmed, to the exact
degree desired by the owner or tenant.

It was discovered, by the pioneers of the world, who
studied all of the complicated questions, which, at
one time, harassed humanity, that the real reason why
we had advanced so slowly, and had remained so
long in the animal stage, was on account of our being
obliged to devote nearly every waking moment to
fight for the mere maintenance of existence. How
could one improve, when one-third of his time was
spent in sleep, and the other two-thirds in labor
necessary to procure the means to provide food, cloth-
ing and shelter? The nervous exhaustion—the wear
and tear of humanity, under a system which required
the expenditure of such vast energies for such trivial
results—made life, for a long time, a very gloomy one.
Happiness was very remote, with only an occasional
glimpse of it being found by the struggling masses.

After the municipality had settled the question of

light and heat and shelter, it took up the question of food. The minds of the best men in the community were directed to the problem of providing for the nourishment of the human body in a more scientific and refined way than the coarse one employed, for so many years, of gathering together the crude forms of carbon, in the shape of raw meat and vegetables, which, under the cover of various forms of roasting devices, were transformed into what was known as the food of that time. So crude and expensive were these methods, that the majority of mankind was bowed down with the hours of labor necessary to pay for the food, which was so gross in its form, and so badly prepared, in the average household, that it was rare to find a person with good health and with perfect digestion. The physicians of that time were a necessary evil, appertaining to that crude form of supplying food to the human machine. Nearly every case in the hands of the physicians could be traced back to over-eating or some corresponding indulgence of the appetite. The moment the manner of supplying the waste to the human machine was discovered, physicians became needless ; and only a limited number of surgeons were able to exist, looking after the accidents which occasionally befell the inhabitants of these ideal communities.

It might be said that no one would work if he did not have the burden of necessity compelling him. This was an argument which was presented to the municipality. When it took up the food question, a commission of scientific gentlemen worked, for many years, and, finally, developed an enormous variety of foods for the maintenance of the existence of humanity. These foods were in the form of liquid preparations, which had the palatable character of the finest wines ; and of tablets, which had the agreeable taste of the most delicate and artistic of French dishes of the highest class. The pleasure of the palate was preserved, without the human frame being called upon to digest the superfluous and gross material, which is, now, pitchforked, three times a day, into the human stomach. The municipality furnished this food, at cost, to the community ; so that, instantly, one of the greatest burdens could be lifted. It was at this time argued that it would be unwise to furnish food at the cost of its production to the community, as the last incentive to material industry would be thus removed.

This question was first taken up and considered by the municipality of New York. All discussions of a character relating to the public took place in the Forum. The Forum was located upon the Palisades. Here was a vast amphitheatre, inside the Forum, capable of seating 100,000 people. Here the arguments of the orators of the day were permitted. The means employed to convey, swiftly, to the minds of the great host there assembled were very ingenious. It is only upon rare occasions that so many people came, as the newspapers of that day published each argument in full, and so every one who could read had an opportunity of following the minds of the municipal directors, in their attempt to advance the interests of the community. The speeches of the orators were taken down with rapidity, and, through a system of electrical connection, their actual words were flashed upon the walls which ran around the amphitheatre, so that those who were at too distant a point to hear fully, could understand everything that was said. Everything relating to the public had to be conducted openly. There was a series of small forums throughout the municipality for the transaction of minor divisions of the business of the community; but, when it came to some great question, involving the rights of the whole, then the meeting was called in the central forum, and there came the municipal council, an august body of honorable men, whose high character made them objects of esteem and reverence in the community.

Twelve citizens of the municipality had a right to summon any official to judgment in the central forum, where he defended himself before a court of honor. The decision of the court of honor was, then, submitted, directly, to the public. He who was ruled against by public opinion received no other punishment than being disqualified, for a period of years, from holding an office of trust. To prevent citizens from bringing charges upon trivial or malicious grounds, it was also provided that, where the petitioners were actuated by dishonest or improper motives in bringing the charges, they should be disqualified, for a period of years, from holding any position of trust, and should be, forever, disqualified from having a right to summon any official to judgment in the forum.

It was found, upon actual experience, that the furnishing of food at cost by the municipality to the community did great good, instead of harm. It was made clear that men, who struggled fiercely to satisfy mere animal demands, work even better to satisfy the higher claims of their nature, when the coarser and commoner ones are no longer obligatory subjects of thought. A spirit of honor, of kindness, and proud emulation, in each community, was developed, to an extraordinary degree, on the day that the toiling sons of man were freed from the centuries-old burden of struggling for food, shelter and clothes.

The country had, now, become so thickly built up, that the people in the country, through the improvements in the method of communication, were made, practically, members of the various municipalities throughout the country. In regions too distant for such service the State took the place of the municipality. The transportation lines, in every direction, were controlled by the Government, so that the rates of travel were reduced to a minimum degree of cost. The Government had become, to a certain extent, the great central trust, occupied with the benevolent intention of reducing, so far as it could, the cost of living.

The graduates of the municipality became candidates for the State Legislatures, and those, in turn, were considered eligible to the National Legislature. The great office of President was held only by a man who had been through the consecutive steps of legislative requirements; and, even then, before he could be considered more than an ordinary candidate, he was required to make a complete circuit of the world, studying over again the lessons of acquirement of

various governments of the earth, before coming to
the high place of chief executive of an ideal nation.
His term was ten years, and he was not eligible to a
re-election. After retiring from that office, he was
made the member of a high court of honor, which sat in
perpetual session at the National Capitol, for the purpose of hearing all charges made against any official
holding place under the Central Government. The
highest crime to be charged against a public official was
that he had neglected the interest of the public, and
the severest punishment was the disapproval of the
public, and his retirement from the position of trust,
with future disqualification for a qualified term of
years.

The key to all this advancement came, however,
first, from individual effort, which preceded the effort
of the municipality, and the acts of the higher forms
of government, to raise up the weaker and more
unfortunate members of society.

The first movement in the direction of eliminating
poverty and suffering from the world came through
the united action of the well-to-do and prosperous.
Societies were formed upon this basis:

Each member of the Society for Adults pledged
himself, during his life, to give his aid and loving care
to one unfortunate person.

Each member of the Society for the Aid of Children
pledged himself to educate, properly train, and develop,
physically, some one helpless child.

As the well-to-do greatly outnumber the wretched,
the destitute and the unhappy, the world-wide union

of the better element soon made an arm of strength
for the poor, until there was no such thing as destitu-
tion, nor absolute want, left in the world. The schools
of crime disappeared, and, in an atmosphere of loving
kindness, evil, gradually, began to give way, and the
era of cruel punishments and savage executions for
crime became things of the past.

CHAPTER XIX.

GENERAL STARR BECOMES A PROSELYTE TO THE DOCTRINES ADVOCATED BY CAPTAIN HARCOURT.

I now found some difficulty in the way of going on with my regular work. I had received several letters of admonition from my editor. It was very confusing, this mingling of the ideal and the real. The ideal—the possible—took away the interest from the petty incidents of ordinary political life. During the day, I went about as before; but every evening I was in Captain Harcourt's rooms, talking with him, or to my immortal soul.

One thing made a distinct impression upon me, and that was the fact that I, myself, had no power of summoning my immortal part and that it was only in Captain Harcourt's presence that he became visible. When away from the Captain, I sometimes wondered if it was not a skillful illusion upon his part—if he did not possess rare powers of producing hallucinations. But I did not long pursue this train of thought, for, if it were an illusion, it was such an agreeable one that I would not forego its delights for any pleasure of a more material kind. But, yet, I was not happy. When engaged in actual conversation with my soul, I was supremely contented; but, when away from the scene where his presence could be invoked, I felt strangely dull and lifeless. It gave me a helpless feeling to be conscious of the fact, at one time of the day, of having an immortal partner, and then, at another time, to find that I did not possess the slightest power of communicating with him.

Soon after the retirement of Ralph Granger from the Cabinet, I found that Captain Harcourt was the center of attraction for many people. He began to have as many callers as a Cabinet officer. I think this all grew out of Madame Neville's knowledge of the Captain's acquirements. He had gone to her house in response to the invitation given him at the ball at the Russian Legation. He interested, deeply, the curious Parisian lady, and she was the means of spreading his fame to such a degree, that, at the time I now speak of, he was besieged by callers, the greater number being ladies. The principal proselytes to any new cult are invariably women, because they have more time on their hands, and are more anxious to cultivate new sensations.

By some, Captain Harcourt was called an out-and-out spiritual medium. Others spoke of him as an occultist, a psychical expert, a theosophist, an astrologer, a teller of fortunes; and, again, by others, the prince of charlatans and of superlative humbugs.

Yet, there must have been some strange power back of him to thus concentrate the attention of polite Washington upon his modest individuality, as he had lived in comparative retirement, and had never made any claim to possess any supernatural powers or gifts.

Of the many callers, all went away enthusiastic from

his presence, although he had but little to say to any one; and, in all his intercourse with his many questioners, he never affected any air of mystery. Yet, he nearly always said the right word, and made the suggestion that brought relief to the countenance shaded by sorrow or doubt. People who came to him, hoping to gain some knowledge concerning the future, never received any satisfaction. But, in all that related to the present, he was an adviser of such unquestioned superiority, that, soon, his time was taxed to the uttermost with the burden of the confidences thrust upon him from every direction.

"This," said he to me, "only proves the restlessness and dissatisfaction with the material conditions of ordinary life. At the first suggestion of real spirituality, that comes free from suspicion, the entire race of man turns its head, like a flower towards the sun. Everybody wants to believe in the higher immortality, and is never sadder than when under the influence of arguments tending to disprove such existence."

One day, General Starr asked me to present him to Captain Harcourt. The old General said: "I have heard a great many stories concerning Captain Harcourt. I have long wanted to meet some man, sincere and honest, who can answer me certain questions concerning another life. Religion, as it has been taught, has never satisfied me. Politics, the world in which I live, is empty and unsatisfactory, when it should be the one where every noble ambition should be gratified."

When General Starr was presented to Captain Harcourt, it was at one of our quiet evening gatherings.

The General went straight to the mark at the outset, by saying :

"Captain Harcourt, my friend here has told me a great deal about you of late, and of the ideal republic. I had, too, my ideals, when I first entered public life. Every honest man has. All novitiates in a public career think of the interests of the public and not their own. But, how can one contend against a system that breeds selfishness, and bids us call forth every active effort of self preservation in order not to be crushed."

To this the Captain replied: "No system can be changed by the efforts of any one man. But that does not change one's duty. It is the duty of each man to live up to the best there is within, regardless of consequences. This you have done, General Starr, as your poverty now shows. You have unswervingly adhered to the path of duty as you have seen it, and if there were more men like you in the public service, the advance of the nation would be greater and more rapid."

When Captain Harcourt took up the question of the immortal soul as the key-note of human advancement, General Starr said : "I am too old-fashioned to go into any such topic as that. If you were to present me to my immortal soul, as you have my friend here, I should not believe it, even if I should see with my own eyes and hear with my own ears. But all this does not prevent me from believing that you, yourself, are sincere, and that you have a great influence in certain directions. I believe certain impressionable people regard you as the prophet of a new religion. As the leader of a new religion, I can treat with you, as I would with any rec-

ognized force met by me in politics.   I want your assistance in seeking to influence the President."

"In seeking to influence the President?" I asked, in
surprise.

"Yes; that is it. All human influences of an ordinary
kind have failed to control him.   Now, if Captain Harcourt, with his army of worshipers, fails, we will have
to give him up."

Captain Harcourt turned, with an air of attention, as
General Starr continued: "When Senator Norton
fell ill, the primary cause was a deep mortification
over the thought that the President had conquered him
and had made him powerless.   Mrs. Ray was the occasion of his break-down.   The proposed duel, and
ridicule consequent upon it, he could have soon thrown
off; but Colonel Wren, the President's private secretary, employed detectives to work up the case of Senator Norton and Mrs. Ray, and then an unofficial person went to the Senator, and told him that if he dared
to raise his head in defiance to the President again,
he would be crushed.   At this very time, the Senator was deeply pained at Mrs. Granger's death, having
learned of Mrs. Ray's visit to the Granger house.   He
broke with her summarily, and so furnished the President with additional weapons—as Mrs. Ray, with her
knowledge of official life and its intrigues, is an enemy
to be feared by any man.   She has now joined the
President's forces, and Senator Norton, who is still de-
lirious from fever, is being enmeshed in the folds of a
combination, which will certainly ruin him, unless the
President be brought to relent.   Now, Captain Har-

court, can't you find, among the ladies who come to you, some one adroit enough to cut the claws of that she-cat Ray, and disarm the President at the same time? The entire political history of this winter's administration begins and ends in this fight between the President and Senator Norton over a few offices. How many lives are yearly lost and ruined in such struggles, the general public would hardly believe."

"What would you have me do?"

"Cultivate the President, and use your own judgment. He has, recently, heard a great deal about you, and, the other day, I heard him express a desire to see you. He is very superstitious, and has heard such exaggerated stories concerning your powers, that he is disposed to give you a large credit. I dare say he would like to ask you about the possibility of a renomination.

"Now, joking aside," continued the General, "I am myself interested in you and your theories concerning the future of our nation. God knows we need higher influences in our political life. It is a cruel cut-throat fight, at present, between ambitious individuals, and the public—to use a common expression—is not in it. How can a public man find time to perform his duty, when he has to be on the continuous defense against a set of men seeking to pull him down and capture his place? If any of us ever have a real desire to do unselfish things, and try to serve the public, who will give us credit? Such acts are construed as acts of weakness, or as bids for popularity based upon presidential ambitions. The truth is: as old a hand as I am, I have never yet found any particular opportunity to do anything really amounting to anything. I may have been of some service to a few individuals, and I have found, besides my own bread and butter, a small slice of fame. That comprises my record. It looks more pretentious than that in the *Congressional Directory*, I know. Now, permit me to ask you a few questions, based upon the information given me by my friend."

"Do you claim to possess any supernatural powers or gifts?"

"None whatever."

"In other words, what you can do is within the range of possibility of any one?"

"Most assuredly."

"You, as I am informed, allege that you see your soul as an individual, and, through him, see things as they really are. You learn, from this higher self, rules of conduct, which, you say, if applied to our national life, would advance our standard of civilization, and give us public men, more satisfactory and more worthy objects of our ambition. Now, in what way are you different from any professional teacher of religion or morals?"

"In theory, not much different. In practice, you might find the code of the Island of Nolos slightly different."

"I will not go into that, for the moment, but will come to the practical application of the superiority you have acquired in your studies. For the moment, I concede your superiority in spiritual and moral power to be all my friend has described it to be. But,

in what way have you been able to help him? He
had, really, great faith that, in attempting to save his
friend, Granger, if he failed in every ordinary direction, in you he would find the extraordinary means
which might be employed."

"I had no power. I pretended to have none. I cannot set aside the results of an event, behind which is a
chain of logically predisposing causes. I have never
assumed the power to change human destinies. Life
can be influenced or controlled at the beginning of one
of its chapters, but the only miracles are those which
men accomplish within themselves. Each man, according to Doctor Longman, can know his higher self as
an individual guide. If he chooses to follow his advice, he will be wise."

"How does your idea of the soul-control differ from
the religious idea of conscience?"

"In theory, it does not differ. But our belief and
practice make the conscience, if you will, a practical,
visible force. All the great accomplishments of men
come from their higher development."

"In what you propose, do you seek to antagonize
existing religious forms?"

"In no way. We do not seek to drive out anything
that does good, or which lives up to its honest profes-
sions. Organized religious societies do great good;
but they all need remodeling, simplifying. They
should all go back to first principles. Let them follow
more closely the doctrines of their faith, and let them,
above all, concentrate their attention upon the poor
and the outcast. When Doctor Longman's belief be-

gins to spread, you will find only a live, modern
agency, ready to co-operate heartily with every form
of organized good, while it will, at the same time, cut
mercilessly at humbug or pretense, no matter under
what name of holiness it may be hiding."

"Give me a practical illustration of what you propose to do."

"First and foremost, to form a chain of societies devoted to love, charity, kindness towards our
fellows; in other words, universal brotherhood. No
form of belief should be required after accepting
the sole requirement of the order of brotherhood—
to love his fellows. A member may believe in one
God or twenty, and he may not believe in God
at all, as he is theologically taught. All we ask is
intellectual honesty, and no hypocrisy. We will
establish throughout the world, great temples which
shall always be open, well warmed and lighted. No
poor person shall ever be denied a shelter under
their roofs. In these temples there will always be
found, night or day, members of the society, ready
to advise or instruct those who seek for information
or aid. They must be beautiful, for in nothing are
the poor so starved as they are of the beautiful. In
them and their divisions there will be schools, where
everything relating to the comfort, the economies,
and the true pleasures of life, will be taught; and,
at intervals, during the day and evening, there should
be beautiful music. Look at the churches of to-day
—great fortresses, representing millions of capital, but
closed during the greater part of the time, and, with

the single exception of the Catholic Church, never open for the poor."

"Would you have sermons?"

"The world has had enough sermonizing. We would have no dull expositions of dead creeds, but lectures upon the art of living, correct thinking, and the true way to arrive at human happiness. These lectures should be made by our most eloquent members. We would make a wide departure from the churches, in that we should always have our temples open to free discussions. Every speaker should be prepared to sustain his views against all comers. Discussion would be invited. One-sided discourses invite intellectual stagnation, while the clash of intellectual strife is the most quickening of influences to the spirit. You will find Doctor Longman intensely practical. He labors to form the intelligent and the well-to-do of this world into such a compact organization, that they can, by such union, abolish crime, poverty and suffering."

The eyes of the old soldier flashed. "I don't care for your mystical side—this meeting of the immortal soul," said he, "but I am with you on your practical side. You can count on me as one of your society members, if you can only make it stick to the code you lay down; but, I fear, a very long time will pass before you will gain over the following necessary to make any real impression upon the sin, suffering and poverty in this world. I am proud that I have enough emotion left in me to be impressed by your plans."

Captain Harcourt replied: "It will take some time; but, perhaps, not so long as you think. People throughout the world are weary of the husks of religion, and are looking more for its real spirit and essence. The day for the threshing of dogmas is rapidly passing. The world, already, is asking, not what a man believes, or professes to believe, but what he really is. Those who lead in this enterprise cannot fail, General Starr, because——"

" Because ?"

" Because the leaders are guided, and will be guided, by their souls. Only those who are in close and intimate daily communication with their individual souls shall be founders of this order!"

The conversation went on for some time, the General saying, as he finally arose to go: "Captain Harcourt, you have made a convert of me, and have taught me what I had long ceased to believe—that there was any real object in life. If you could impress the President, as you have impressed me, you might, perhaps, persuade him to renounce his obstinacy, and to give up his contentions with his associates. If we really had a high-minded President in the White House, who followed the code of the Island of Nolos, then, perhaps, he might influence some of us public men to give a more loyal following to his executive suggestions."

CHAPTER XX.

GENERAL STARR AND CAPTAIN HARCOURT TALK OF THE EVIDENCES OF ANOTHER LIFE. DOES DEATH END ALL?

I had been so occupied in following the pictures of an ideal world, that I had quite neglected the real one, where I had had most active duties to perform. I now received a long letter of complaint from the chief editor of my newspaper. He said I was losing my sense of news values. I had passed over the most sensational matter in the most perfunctory fashion. My absence of interest in current things he could not account for, unless I was ill, or beginning to run down. As he was a personal friend, he criticised me with all possible gentleness. He advised me to take three months' vacation, and seek a change of scene.

But I refused to go away. I accepted the vacation from my work, but decided to remain with my friend, and watch the growth of the founding of the new movement, that embraced in it so many features of the doctrines of Theosophy, without any of the apparent mysteries of that cult, as it had been taught. There was a simplicity and a directness about Captain Harcourt's methods that constantly attracted me.

Yet, in spite of what I had seen and felt in his

presence, away from him, doubts would come. Nothing made a greater impression upon me, at this time, than a story related to me by General Starr, giving an actual experience of his with an officer of his command.

The question came up on another occasion, when General Starr called upon Captain Harcourt to invite him to go with him, upon the following evening, to call upon the President. The latter was anxious to see Captain Harcourt, and the details of the arrangement for a meeting at the White House were made, without difficulty, by the General.

After the talk upon this subject was completed, the General said: "You speak so confidently, Captain Harcourt, about death and another life, I wish you would explain to me an incident that occurred during the year following the war. A staff-officer of mine, who settled down near me as a neighbor, fell ill, one severe winter day, with pneumonia. To all appearance, he died, and was buried. The night of his burial his body was stolen from its grave, a country cemetery, by a band of medical students, and his body carried straight to the dissecting table of our town hospital. Just as the knives were about to be plunged into the corpse, my friend opened his eyes, and asked for a drink of water. After a moment of fright, the students rallied about him, and he was, slowly, but surely, brought back to full consciousness. Here was a man who, to all appearances, had died—had been actually buried in the grave, where no air could reach him— and, having died from pneumonia, must have been regarded by the medical men as having absolutely no chance for being a victim of suspended animation. Yet, his description of his own death, and the resultant state, has done more to make me doubt whether there is really another life after this than all the arguments of the straightest of infidels. Now, if you can relieve my mind of that doubt, you will give me a better heart for the religion of my fathers, which I have long professed ; but, in my innermost heart, never have fully believed."

"Go on."

"This is the story he tells of his death. As physical life became low, his brain cleared. All pain had gone. He felt that he was much better. He wanted to tell those about him that he was surely going to get well, but he could not lift a finger, or, even, move his eyelids. He heard every sound in the room. The words of pity from the watchers, concerning his evident misery and suffering, amazed him. Then he heard some one say that the sun was shining in his face, and to drop the curtain. To him the sun had been gone for hours. Then he thought, for the first time, of death, and, then, that he was dying. A delicious languor stole over him. He felt an imperious desire to go to sleep, and even wanted to turn over on his side, but could not move. Then he fell asleep, and became unconscious."

"Well?"

"He did not recover consciousness again until he felt the sensation of thirst upon the dissecting table. Now, mark you, he was, for all practical purposes, dead, and, as a dead man, he slept. When he awoke, he remembered even less than from the slumber of a night. This experience, so clearly and succinctly told, has implanted, in my mind, the thought that death may, after all, be a kind and merciful sleep that knows no wakening. If there is a consciousness afterwards, why did not my friend, whose mind was so clear up to the very last, pierce the veil and seize upon even a fragment of a view of the life beyond?"

"General Starr," said Captain Harcourt, "is that all your logic can find in that incident? Do you not see that the consciousness of the other life did not come because life still clung to the body. The spark of life was low, but it was still there, and so the physical life controlled. Had this spark been actually extinguished, then spiritual consciousness would soon have been awakened. We sink to sleep in death. The first stage of the departure from life was very correctly described by your friend; but, if he had not remained there, then he could not have returned to you as a living witness."

"What do you know about the other life? Oh, I forget: a man who has an immortal double should know something. Well, if you tell me there is another life, and that you know it, then I shall be willing to accept you, at least, as an honest witness."

"I think every sane, honest man can find within himself the proof of his own immortality. It comes from self-study. Nothing created is ever destroyed. There is no exception to the rule of the indestructibility of matter. If matter created is indestructible, then life, which is higher, and controls matter, is equally indestructible. Man can find what he will.

Immersed in material things, we become materialists
and doubters. A man who cultivates his higher and
spiritual side soon learns the irresistible logic of not
only another life, but of a succession of lives. For, in
nature, there is never any rest."

"But, if people are to live over and over again, and
advance upon the upward grade of a higher develop-
.ment, through endless cycles of time, what becomes of
human ties—the home affections? All do not advance
equally."

"You see, in the heavens, countless systems of
stars, moving through space, united and attracted to a
common center, which travels on with the whole vast,
visible host of heavenly bodies, in one solidarity of
movement, that is the wonder of the scientific world.
Everything is in motion ; even the vast Universe moves.
So it is not hard to conceive, in studying this incom-
parable magnificence of the working of divine law, that
countless spirits, attracted about some common center
of affection, move onward along differing lines ; but,
yet, belonging, in the best sense, to each other, as they
did in the lower plane of existence."

"I wish I could see something of this with my own
eyes," said the General. "The other night, I said that
I did not want to ; but, now, I believe, I have the
courage to face my own soul, and be very grateful to
you if you can convince me that I have one."

"You express a wish that should exist with every
one. I know of no more important question than the
one which concerns a future life. Men toil and struggle
in this world to find comfort and happiness in a brief

space of earthly existence; but the majority of them ignore questions directed to this subject of vital importance—do we live again? Yet, as with subjects outside of the routine, people who give much attention to this most important subject in the world are regarded as men of feeble minds, or possessing unsound judgment."

"Cranks," said the General.

"Yes," said the Captain; "the subject of another life must be pursued under the cover of the Church— under the direction of the organized clergy—in order to command respect. But what does the Church teach? That the spirits who return to the earth are devils, and that only danger can result from the study of such subjects. So great is the public prejudice outwardly displayed, that the people who might give evidence of a valuable character are discredited in every possible way. Now, all this will be changed in the future."

"In what way?"

"Some day this will become a great public question. The work of the Society for Psychical Research is preparing the way for it. Some day, public moneys will be voted for the conduct of such investigations. Congress has given thousands of dollars to find the path to the North Pole—why should it not appropriate money for an honest research to prove or disprove the existence of another world than this?"

"Well, that is an idea." The General laughed. "I can imagine the sensation that would be created if a bill to that effect were to be introduced in the Senate.

Such a senator would be, undoubtedly, classed as a lunatic."

"Unquestionably; but, every day, money is appropriated for idler objects, and no one questions."

"That is because the money is to be sent for accustomed objects, even if such spending is often regarded as idle waste. Yet, you will see, in the future enlightened years, money spent by the Government in just such directions. People divinely gifted will, then, be objects of care and protection. They will be freed from the care of money-getting, and surrounded by every aid to uphold their honesty and truthfulness. No one ever need be afraid of the truth, wherever found. Spiritual investigations, put in high hands, conducted in the open light of public criticism and observation, would result in something practical. Every man in the civilized world really wishes to believe in his immortal part, and every one would welcome proofs coming to him from high and unquestionable sources. But, still, the greatest evidence of another life will not come from this source. It will only prepare the .way for the absolute proof, which will be given to the world by the scientists."

"By the scientists?"

"The scientific men are the salt of the earth. To them the human race owes more than to all its so-called spiritual advisers. These gentlemen have one watchword, viz., 'the truth'; and but one motto, and that is, 'prove all things.'"

"In what way will the scientists be able to give the absolute evidence of another life beyond this?"

"In the simplest possible way. The development of modern science, already, is upon the track of conducting electricity upon the waves of the ether of the Universe, so that messages have been clearly sent for short distances without the medium of wires. Well, this system will be completed in time, so that we will be able to receive messages from the neighboring planets which are inhabited."

"But, suppose that were true, how could we understand the language of the messages?"

"The intelligence of the scholars of modern times, which has learned, with ease, to read the hieroglyphics of the cuneiform period, would find it a light task to read the language of the superior races, upon the higher planes of other planet life. From the experience of the life of a people who have passed through the grade of animalism, in which the earth still dwells, we would soon learn to measure the littleness of our present methods, and the degrading selfishness of the ordinary pursuits of the being known as man."

"Well, I am sure, I should be delighted to read such messages, if they were honestly recorded. I fancy, however, that it would take a very strong corps of savants to convince the United States Senate that there was any body of men anywhere in the Universe that could teach them lessons in wisdom."

Here, the General continued : "Some way, your voice has such a convincing accent. Almost without knowing why, I am ready to believe all you say, as if you were an actual witness of the things you assert so dogmatically. Heavens! what an experience it would be to occupy a seat in a Senate, where the gifts of office and the spoils of power were brushed away, and where great questions and unselfish issues, alone, could obtain. I could face the quest of my immortal soul with infinite patience, Captain Harcourt; why can't you do as much for me as you have for my friend?"

To this the Captain only replied: "Wait."

And the General added: "All things come to him who has learned to stand and wait."

CHAPTER XXI.

I INVOKE, ALONE, MY SOUL AND RECEIVE SOME DI-RECTIONS FOR SPIRITUAL DEVELOPMENT.

This story, in all its bearings, must, of a necessity, center about Captain Harcourt, who came to this country as the prophet of a new cause. The propagation of his teachings explains, to a degree, the sudden passion for doing good that is now so rapidly being developed among us. If this movement increases in the future with rapidity similar to that of the last five years, there will come a time, predicted by my friend, when the poor and desolate will become so few in number, that there will not be enough left to occupy the rapidly growing host of philanthropists. In nothing was he so impressive and emphatic as in his teaching the doctrine of kindness and charity.

"In no other way," said he, "can the difference between classes be modified. Through no other means can labor and capital be reconciled. The exercise of the brute power of might must pass. Neither are we to keep all of our charity for the poor. Many of the rich are in as dire need of help. In life there are the two extremes of unhappiness and happiness. Each person is rightfully entitled to happiness. A rich man, deprived of happiness, is quite as much an object of charity as the poor man. He stands quite as much in need of being directed and taught how to live, as his, apparently, more unfortunate brother."

In his visit to Washington, the Captain sought to interest those who were in such positions of authority, that the effect of their conversion should have the widest influence. So it was with pleasure that he looked forward to his visit to the President. He had never, so far as I had heard, introduced any one to his soul by the direct means employed with myself. He had always stopped short upon the threshold of possibility, leaving the seeker interested by suggestions of a future beyond the material environments that surround us. "For," said he, "unless you can have this hope before you, then unselfishness is foolish. There is no longer any reason for not crushing your fellow, and the obtaining, by fair or foul means, the means for maintaining a footing of superiority in a world marked by the exact limitations of the cradle and the grave. But the moment you concede a future existence, then the reasons for the opposite course are equally clear. How important, therefore, to see clearly!"

"Will you introduce the President to his soul, when you go to see him?"

"Yes. He will see him once. Whether again or not, will depend upon his will. I shall present to him a view of his real surroundings, and, in so doing, I shall give him the point of comparisons, by showing some of the possibilities of his great office, as the chief magistrate of one of the most powerful nations of the world."

When evening came of the day that the Captain was

to go to the White House, he sent for me, and told me that I had permission to go with him.

"But," said I, "the President would not consent. He would rather give up seeing you, than to run the risk of having a word about it in the newspapers."

"I know that. But you are not writing now, and I bring you there as my associate. I am beginning to find great help in you, and as I wish to make, during this night, the final demonstrations devised by Doctor Longman, I wish you to be with me and make full observations of what is done. For, when this night is passed, I must be on my way elsewhere, leaving the threads of the undeveloped work in your hands."

"You are going away?" said I, in alarm.

"Yes; and at once. To-morrow; but I shall remain in constant communication with you. If your faith is strong, you will have at hand the means of happiness. That is a cult you will learn in time; but I warn you that if your faith wavers, you will, in the end, be more unhappy than before. Then your only safety will be to go at once to the Island of Nolos, and place yourself in the hands of Doctor Longman, whose strength is greater than mine by an hundred fold. I have given you the best counsel that is within me, but I am but a novice in the initiation of others to the mystery of direct soul-communication. You should be successful in seeing your own soul, unaided, by this time. Once you reach that point, then you will have an ally against doubt. But, in working alone, you must not expect to reach at once the same success you have had with the aid of my strength. You have time to try the experiment this evening, as we are not to go to the White House before midnight. Go, now, to your own room, and evoke the visual presence of your own soul."

"But how can I do that? What directions shall I follow?"

"Go to your room, sit down quietly, and wait. Take the Egyptian mirror with you; keep your eyes fixed tranquilly upon its surface, and do not be too anxious. Be calm and patient. I will help you from here; but, if you succeed now, you will have less difficulty when I am at a distance."

I went back to my room, lighted my gas, and sat down in front of my writing-table, under the central light of the room. I placed the mirror at the right of a mass of blank white paper. I picked up a pen, dipped it in the ink, and idly gazed upon the dark mirror as I sketched, loosely, the fragmentary heads that steal out so easily from under a pen held in an idle hand. Suddenly, my arm stiffened, and I was thrilled by the sensation of a foreign control of my arm. I had heard of automatic writing, but I had never thought, for a moment, that I possessed any such ability. It was with a thrill of expectation that I felt my muscles acting under the direction of an unseen influence. Suddenly, my arm became rigid, and the pen began to move awkwardly. A few clumsy marks were made, and then words began to form. I watched, with eager attention. In a moment, the following was written:

"Don't believe all you see."

Here was a shock to my belief, and, as my hand continued to form words and phrases, I found nothing in them of point, sense or meaning. As I tossed the pen aside, with impatience, I felt doubts again stealing over me. What was all this juggling with absurdities? Then, suddenly, came to my mind the memory of a man, a former friend, who had become insane. His first symptom of aberration, as described by his physician, was the aimless scribbling of faces and meaningless phrases upon every scrap of paper within his reach. But all this was not obeying Captain Harcourt's request. I fought away the doubts, the fear of the ridicule that follows upon the heels of the unusual, and turned to the mirror. I looked, long and patiently, but it was an hour before I saw any change upon its surface. Then the gray shadows began to form, and a spirit of tranquility took possession of me.

Then, after a few moments, I saw, in the depths of the dull, black surface of the mirror, the shadowy outlines of my second self. After a time, the vision in the mirror faded, and I saw, seated near me, my soul, but not presenting the solidity of form shown when I had met him in the rooms of Captain Harcourt.

He was now a transparent, gray, shadowy form, and no word from him reached my ear. But to my consciousness there came the answers to my questions, in quite as clear a way as if we had used ordinary speech. Almost the first thing said to me by my soul, was this:

"You began wrong when you came to this room to invoke my presence."

"You mean the surrender of my hand to a seeming automatic control of an unknown force?"

"Yes; never surrender one bit of your individuality to any influence outside of yourself, except under conditions of permission that can be rigidly controlled by your will. In ignoring this condition lies all the evil of spiritual investigations. There is no subject in the world so harmful as the investigation of spiritual phenomena, unless careful conditions are observed. Its laws will, ultimately, be made clear by the scientific world, so that the blunders and evils brought about by ignorant investigation will be avoided. You, in sitting here, allowed, without thought, your hand to be seized upon, and the result was a meaningless gabble, brought to you by the rush of low spiritual elements, which always seek to control when the physical control of an individual is surrendered. Preserve your own individuality always. Observe, in any study of the immaterial world, carefully, the rule of cultivating only what shall contribute to your own spiritual advancement. Such cultivation is not found in mixed assemblages, but rather in solitude. When one is alone, he should give his thoughts to the best that there is within him, as such thoughts attract to him the influences of the good, and so great results are often accomplished, beyond the natural capacity of the seeker. Remember, all the great workers and leaders of the world are those who, while in earnest sympathy with their fellows, yet have matured all that there is of the good and great within them, in self-communion and solitude."

"Do you mean that one does not gain by association with his fellows?"

"There is a loss and a gain. But no man can

achieve greatness who has not learned the art of living
to himself, nor can he develop to the plane of greatness without the fructifying influences of solitude.
Nearly all of the great men in history owe their
strength to country breeding. The city saps the vital
personality, the individual man, no matter how it may
train him in the sharp discipline of its hurried strivings. No man can hold his force and escape deteriora-
tion, who does not keep in close touch with nature
and her wholesome surroundings. To cultivate the
spirituality that surrounds one's self, is to strengthen,
to the highest degree, the possibilities of one's nature.
To seek to cultivate this same spirituality through
vulgar means of the interpretation of others, is at once
a surrender of one's own individuality and a loss."

"By this you mean that each person holds within
himself the full power to receive the messages of the
other world, and to develop, within the limits of his
own individuality, all that is necessary to be known to
prove the existence of another life?"

"That is my meaning. The material phenomena of
Spiritualism should always be investigated by scientific
people of careful and well-established reputations,
under kindly and favoring conditions. Their reports,
alone, can have any value as evidence. There is a
class, and there will be, for some time, who wish to
have material evidence of the existence of another life;
but, I repeat, the best evidence is what one finds himself, and within himself. The greatness of any individual is measured exactly by his capacity to receive."

"If that were fully understood and believed, men

would have selfish reasons for devoting their lives to the highest development of their natures."

"If you look at the various causes which make this or that man stand out superior to his fellows, you will find, nearly always, the reason to be, admittedly, outside of himself. In all the callings of life, in which beauty is the underlying motive, such as music, poetry, or the arts, you have inspiration conceded by every one. To say that a poet, a musician, or an artist, is inspired, is to pay him the highest of compliments, and one that even the most prejudiced in spiritual matters accepts as a compliment. If the world believes in inspiration in these higher matters, it is logical that inspiration—that is, help from a higher source—can be had for every walk of life, provided one places himself in the way of receiving such help."

"You could have, then, according to your view, an inspired day laborer."

"Certainly."

"What should one do to place himself in the way of receiving such help?"

"It is simple, and yet difficult. One should cultivate, first of all, great tranquility of the mind. Employ every agency to avoid misfortune; but bear, patiently, what cannot be avoided. Avoid inharmonious companionships—everything that has a tendency to fetter or degrade the individuality. Live simply, and cultivate your powers of perception, so that you can have, always, an occupation for the mind, to save it from falling into harassing ruts. A man who thinks, steadily, of the happiness and comfort of others is on the high road to happiness and comfort himself. Avoid all unkindness, as you would the plague. Live, as much as you can, in the open air, and in the sun. The man who has fully developed his individuality, and who has fortified it against doubt or worry, is a fortress against the inroad of the enemy, disease."

As this last injunction was being flashed upon my inner consciousness, the gray shadow of my better self faded, and I heard nothing more.

I glanced at my watch. It was nearly midnight. It was time to join Captain Harcourt, and go with him to the White House, where he proposed to make the final demonstrations of the doctrines of the Island of Nolos, before his departure from Washington.

CHAPTER XXII.

SHOWING THE FUTURE GOVERNMENT OF AFFAIRS IN THE UNITED STATES.

We arrived at the White House about midnight. We were shown up to the library-room, where I was admitted, with General Starr, upon the occasion of our visit to the President, in the interests of Ralph Granger.

This time there was no supper ; but upon a near side-board were to be found comfortable, black bottles, flanked by open boxes of cigars. In the room, with the President, were the members of his Cabinet, the Speaker of the House, the Vice-President, and a round dozen of senators and members, the real leaders upon whom the President depended when he wanted anything done. The Chief Justice of the Supreme Court, with several of his associates, was also present. The three branches of the Government were thus well represented.

The active host upon this occasion was Colonel Wren, the President's private secretary. It was he who received us, and made known the President's wishes. He desired to make an explanation of Captain Harcourt's character, so that what he proposed to do should be made known to those present, as he had indicated no special object in the invitations he had sent out for the private conference.

Colonel Wren, after we were seated, arose and, turning to the group of assembled dignitaries, said : " The President has asked you to come here this evening for the purpose of witnessing an experiment, which he has been given to understand Captain Harcourt is ready and anxious to make. You all know, or have heard of, Captain Harcourt. His powers are said to be wonderful. The President has been anxious to witness the evidence of his ability, and has thought that you, who are his special friends, would be interested."

All now turned towards Captain Harcourt. From the puzzled look upon several faces, it was evident that all had not heard of him. The President had formed the habit of inviting his friends among the officials at Washington to come to the White House after midnight, as the then President never retired before three or four o'clock in the morning. He was fond of amusement, and when a bountiful supper was not the excuse for the gathering, then it was to meet the most notable lion in the amusement world, who might chance to be in Washington. So it was quite in accordance with his habit to be acting as the host of such a noteworthy person as Captain Harcourt.

The latter arose at the brief introduction of Colonel Wren, and bowed gravely. He first saluted the President, and addressed to him his remarks. He said :

" Mr. President, I propose, in the briefest possible fashion, to indicate what I propose to do, and, as I proceed, I ask only to have your undivided attention. You and your guests present will not question the declaration that our Government, as constituted, falls far behind the ideal of those who projected it. I am, if you please, a reformer—a not over-popular character in Washington. But the reforms I propose are those you will be willing to undertake. I am the representative of a society which teaches its members to see things as they are, as well as how they should be, and by such sight lay the foundation for a higher civilization. Government has no excuse, unless it is framed for the equal protection of the wealthiest and humblest members of society. Can any of you gentlemen honestly say that such is the ideal of our Government to-day?"

None of the officials present condescended to reply. The President began to look bored. After all, what if Captain Harcourt should turn out to be only one of those dreaded reformers, whose reforms begin and end with speeches?

Captain Harcourt continued: "No, I have no intention of making a speech. I merely wish to indicate what I hope to show. Instead of saying anything more, I will merely, for the time being, open your eyes and let you see the ideal reign of power. I will begin first with the Congressional branch of the Government, and," here he bowed to the President, "I will come to the Executive branch of the Government as the closing picture."

At the word "picture," the President, who was beginning to doze, waked up and was all attention.

Here Captain Harcourt moved his hand and sat down. As he did so, the lights in the room grew dim. A heavy darkness filled the chamber, the walls of the room disappeared, and then, in a center of light, at first far away, gradually expanding until the guests sat as spectators, looking down upon the ideal House of Representatives, such as I had seen and have described in an earlier chapter.

There was a shout of admiration at the scene. The Speaker murmured: " If your reform follow such noble lines as this you will have many followers."

No one expressed any wonder at the means employed to produce such a scene. All were content to feast their eyes upon the picture, which had a perfect air of reality.

The chamber, which had been empty when I first saw it, now began to fill with splendid-looking men. Then the ideal Speaker took his seat, and at a signal from him the ideal House arose, and then there came marching down the center aisle a separate group of distinguished-looking men, who took seats upon benches in front of the Speaker's desk. These men were announced by their titles. They were the Cabinet advisers of the President, who came to take part in the regular sessions of the House. The President was greatly interested in this feature.

He turned to Captain Harcourt and said: " Is this a correct picture of what will take place in the future?"

" It is," was the reply. " There will be many years of opposition to this change, but it will come in time. One of the chief advantages will be the raising of the character of the Cabinet advisers. These men can no longer be selected through whim or personal favor of a President; for, as they are required to come to the

House to answer questions and to present the wishes of the administration in power, so will its character depend upon the class of men selected. Those who are not able and adroit will be unable to hold their place."

" But," said the President, " I see thirteen members. What additions are those which you have made to exhibit an ideal condition ? "

" The ranking officer in this Cabinet," was the reply, " will be no longer the Secretary of State. I will give you the Cabinet as you see it in the chamber before you. The first Cabinet officer is the Secretary of the Public Welfare. He is immediately charged with the well-being of the citizen. His sole business is to right private wrongs, and to give his entire time to what, in his judgment, will best contribute to the welfare of the individual.

" The next is the Secretary of the Liberal Arts. He is charged with the promotion of culture of beauty in its many forms. He has the power, with rich rewards and prizes, to stimulate to the highest degree all those who have any talent for the arts in any form. It is through this office that the cultivation of beauty, in the varied forms of architecture, sculpture and painting, have been brought to such a pitch of excellence as to give you the splendid work exhibited in the hall into which you are now looking.

" After him, comes the Cabinet as you now have it. This brings up the number to ten. The other three gentlemen are: Secretary of Commerce, of Labor, and, lastly, the Secretary of Spiritual Development. The Secretary of Commerce is charged with all questions of interstate commerce. The Secretary of Labor is the one who regulates all questions arising between labor and capital, while the last is charged with all questions of a spiritual character. It will some day, doubtless, rank all of the other ministers in importance ; but, in the scene which I show you, it comes last, as I do not wish to shock too much your prejudices."

· The Chief Justice here spoke : "All the other positions I can understand, but what do you mean by this last designated office. If you refer to religion, such a creation would not be possible, as the Constitution forbids a State religion or any union of Church and State."

"By this is meant," said Captain Harcourt, "the creation of a department for the investigation of all spiritual questions, without any attempt to establish any dogma, or to even discuss the question of so-called religion. The great question of the existence of another world, whether there is such a thing as a future existence or not, will be considered by this department, and all people gifted with special powers, who can throw any light upon this subject, will be given support by this branch of the Government, so that they need be in no way dependent upon the public. This department will be created just as soon as science has progressed far enough to enable mankind to receive communications from the distant planets. The science of astronomy, now fostered and supported by the Government, will prove the base of this new department. With the improvement in telescopes, you will, in time, see the inhabitants of other worlds, and, when the means of communicating with them is perfected, then you will have such proofs of a future existence that, what now appears so vague and chimerical, will become so practical and real as to justify the formation of this special department."

" But," said the Speaker, "without discussing the merits or demerits of the Cabinet as you present it, I would merely suggest that it will be a long time before this country will see the change which you suggest here, in placing the Cabinet upon the floor of the House. There is a great prejudice in Congress against any such innovation. It has been, often, proposed to have the President's advisers on the floor, and to give them power to take part in the discussions of pending questions, in the fashion of the English Parliament. But, in spite of the arguments for it, there has always been one objection that has overshadowed all of the arguments ever made in its favor. This is, the undue influence that would be exercised by the Executive in influencing legislation. It was the intention of the fathers to keep the three branches of the Government as separate as possible."

" That objection is purely a fanciful one. The power of patronage of office distribution now gives the executive branch of the Government an undue influence upon legislation. This is now all the greater, because exercised secretly. If everything were in the light of open day, subject to the publicity of a free discussion, you would not have such an influence from the Executive to contend against as now. If there was the faintest suggestion of it, it could be instantly exposed

in the daily sessions of the House.   The debates would
gain in interest, and the separation would even become
more distinct than it is at present."

There followed a moment of silence, and then every
one's attention was directed to the Chamber.   A discussion began, as if to illustrate the weakness of the
objection made by the Speaker.   The members began
to question the Cabinet officers concerning their work,
and the fierce examinations made into the work of the
Administration placed every one upon his mettle.   No
Cabinet officer, in pursuit of a blind or selfish cause,
could hold up his head against the arguments that came
from every side from the trained and well-equipped
legislators.

"Every Cabinet officer who fails to sustain himself,"
said Captain Harcourt, "will be compelled to resign,
and seek service again in some humbler position."

The legislators, who had looked with so much
interest upon the discussion in the House, where only
questions of real public interest were permitted by the
Speaker, were now invited to turn their attention to
the Senate chamber.   Here was a grave and dignified
assemblage, sitting as a high court of appeal upon
questions decided in the House.   Rarely were the
decisions of the lower chamber reversed.   The office
question was no longer the principal one here.   All
but the great offices of the Government had been
made elective by the people, and so the subject of
patronage, which now makes the Senate the least
consequential of bodies, so far as mere public interests
were concerned, had forever disappeared.

The senators in the group appeared the least interested in this demonstration, and one of them, a friend of Senator Norton's, said: "Captain Harcourt was right to speak of this as an ideal condition, but one that, in my judgment, can never be realized."

To this the Captain replied: "There you are wrong. When once the public is fully wakened up to the degrading effects of the present system of office distribution as it now exists, it will be abolished, exactly as I have pictured it before you."

The next picture was one that interested, to a great degree, the Chief Justice. It was a scene, which represented a court, where the poorest and humblest citizen of the country who had a claim against the Government, could, without expense to himself, save a small percentage upon the award, and, in the event of success, have the issues of his claim passed upon their merits alone. No question of political influence or social relationship could come here. The sole question allowed to be considered was this: Does the Government owe the money? If it did, the decree always gave the full amount to the last penny, with the interest from the date when the debt was made. A judge was reading a decision, as we sat and watched the action of this high court of justice.

In this opinion, the learned judge held that it was as important for a government to maintain as high a standard of honor, in its relations with private creditors, as with public ones, and that it should be as anxious to pay a just debt due to an individual as to a corporation, or syndicate of subscribers to bond issues. " In plain words," said the judge, "it is the duty of the Government to set up the highest possible standards of honor and justice in its dealings. In no other way can it be loyally and honestly served."

To all this the Chief Justice of the Supreme Court nodded a most vigorous assent.

But this scene shifted, to give way to a still more imposing court scene, where a full bench of wise and honest men sat for the purpose of trying election cases. These judges were the highest paid of all, and they held their places for life. They were held to a rigid accountability by the Court of Honor, which sat once a month for the consideration of charges against all federal officials.

This court of elections was free from all partisanship, and passed upon all federal cases. Disputed election questions in the States came to them only upon appeal.

It was clear that all present recognized the importance and correctness of principle underlying the establishment of such a court.

But, as the Speaker said, "How ideal a picture you are now presenting, Captain Harcourt, we practical politicians alone can comprehend."

"Such a court will be possible," said Captain Harcourt, "when men will scorn to succeed unless they are right, and will take more pride in an honest failure than a dishonest success."

CHAPTER XXIII.

THE IDEAL PRESIDENT HOLDS A CONVERSATION WITH THE REAL PRESIDENT OF THE UNITED STATES.

It was now the turn of the Executive Department. Those present directed their attention to the President, when the scenes described in the last chapter had faded away. There was also a change in the President's demeanor. He was no longer indolent and heavy. Something of his inner nature was awakened, and, for the moment, he looked his position of President of the United States. He arose, straightening himself unconsciously, as he found the eyes of his guests centered upon him. I think that, for a few moments, he was reluctant to face the trial. He had been noted for pursuing anything but an ideal course, and so the comparison with which he was threatened was not one which he would have naturally sought.

He parried for a moment, by asking Captain Harcourt a few questions. He began: " From whence do you obtain your particular power to so hypnotize us as to · compel us to see the things which you create with your will?"

The Captain replied: " It is no hypnotism. It is no compulsion of the will, but rather the opening, for the time being, of your eyes."

"But how is that done?"

"The methods employed are very simple. We live in two worlds—the real world, which you see with your physical eyes, and the ideal, which is seen with the spiritual eyes, or what is commonly called the eyes of the imagination. The real and the spiritual world are close together. I, only, have the power to see both worlds, and, occasionally, to be permitted to show it to others."

"You speak of permission. Who gives you the permission? Who is your superior?"

"The permission comes from the powers of the ideal world; that has no particular personality. I only know when I can and when I cannot."

"But you yet have not told how you exercise this power."

"I do not exercise any power. I am the instrument merely of the power of others. Whether you see or do not see does not depend upon me. I, individually, am able at times to produce the channel of thought, which makes such visions natural and simple. There are those who believe as I, who have individual powers of an extraordinary character. Doctor Longman, of the Island of Nolos, has this power. In one sense, he is my superior officer, and from him I receive instructions, which I am very willing to obey; but he would not compel me, against my will, to do anything. I find it very natural and simple, however, in these matters, to seek his advice, and to yield myself absolutely to his wishes, which are, to me, absolutely, commands."

The President continued: "I have heard that you

have been permitted, if I may use your language, to introduce people to their immortal souls. Now, I think that it would be much more interesting to me if you would first present me to my immortal part, before proceeding to give us the pictures of an ideal direction of the Executive Department."

The Captain said : "There surely can be no objection to that. I have received special directions, and, yielding my consent, I merely voice the affirmation of those who speak through me. It is, however, most agreeable and desirable that you should first express this wish. You occupy the most prominent position in one of the richest and most powerful nations of the world. What you are has a mighty influence, first, upon the thousands who follow and who believe in the chief of their party, and, second, upon those many more thousands who always respect and honor the President of the United States, no matter what may be his shade of political belief."

The President's eyes brightened, and his face assumed a kindly expression in response to the most respectful attitude of Captain Harcourt. He said no more, but stood in an attitude of waiting, as if at a morning reception.

Then there came the same prelude which had heralded the advance of the pictures which had just been shown. The room was darkened for a moment, while faint, wavy lines of light, upon bands of gray, moved, in undulating forms, through the darkness. Then there came a sound of majestic music, a triumphal march, and, then, darkness suddenly parted, and there advanced, in a circle of dazzling light, the ideal President of the United States. The look of calm superiority and dignified strength made the President, for the moment, shrink back, and then he began to study his double with a rapt intensity of expression, which smoothed out all of the trivial lines from his round, smooth, pleasure-loving face. For the moment, everything else was forgotten. He was wholly unconscious of the fact that the guests were busy in comparing the attitude and bearing and manner of the two Presidents which stood before them. The real President was devoted to the accomplishment of his personal ambition. He rarely delegated his authority to any one, unless it could not be avoided. He was particularly jealous of the powers of his office in all that related to personal appointments. His entire time was occupied, therefore, with the details of personal affairs, and it was very rarely that he had leisure requisite for the study of national questions. When a public question was forced upon his attention, that was always delegated to some one of his advisers for the preparation of an opinion, for he could not spare the time from the distribution of appointments, and he occupied all of his brief leisure with calculations concerning the possibilities of his renomination. Every office given by him in these days was used for the purpose of making votes for himself in the Presidential Convention; but he was so long in making up his mind, and so dogged in following his own personal ideas, ignoring, nearly always, the recommendations of every one, that he, in the end, made more enemies than friends with the same appointments.

He was particularly jealous of the powers of the Senate. Other presidents had deferred to suggestions of senators in the appointments in their State ; but this particular President ignored the senators, and was very angry with them if they declined to approve his appointments, insisting that the Constitution gave them no power to reject appointments sent in by him, unless for some grave and serious reasons. He questioned the Senate's right to veto his action, although he, without any hesitation, vetoed their action when it came before him in the form of legislation, without even so much as an apology. The rights given to him by the Constitution he never questioned, and he was ever ready to stretch his privileges to the utmost limit, while, at the same time, he questioned very seriously the constitutionality of many of the privileges of the other branches of the Government, and was always eager to assert his personal powers in controversies with the Senate.

The ideal President had a look, upon his stern, clean-cut face, of a man of high and mighty resolutions. It would be impossible to associate him with questions of individual vanity, or with pursuing selfish purposes. He was a noble, calm, strong-looking man, and yet his features were, in every way, the reproduction of features of this weak, vain and self-opinionated President. It was the high character shining out of his face, however, which made the change, and established the gulf of difference between the two men.

The real President turned to Captain Harcourt, after he had looked at his second self for fully five minutes without speaking, and then he said: "If this is really my immortal part, and is no delusion of the senses, it may be possible that he can speak, and that he can answer certain questions that I would like very much to put to him."

"Any question which you may ask will be answered by him."

The President, who was a very gentlemanly man, now turned with a half bow of apologetic embarrassment to his guests. He would much have preferred to have carried on this conversation without auditors. He first asked:

"Are you really my immortal soul?"

"I am."

"Are you constantly associated with me?"

"I am."

"Do you take part in everything that I do?"

"I do not. It is very rarely that I take part in anything that you do."

"What do you mean by that?"

"Exactly what I say."

"Oh, I forget. You represent the ideal condition of humanity."

"I am the divine part of you. As you reach upward, and seek the diviner part of yourself, and you can only do this by forgetting yourself, then you and I come together, and only then."

The President continued: "Do you have greater opportunities, through being the immortal part of the President of the United States? In other words, does the elevation of an individual, officially, and through his exercising great power, have a tendency to develop his better self?"

A shadow came over the serene face of the ideal, as if, for the moment, he did not comprehend the exact bearing of the President's question. He answered, generally: "The soul of all men is the same; it has no more influence upon the man, against his will, if he happens, by chance, to occupy the body of a President, than if he occupied the body of the humblest workman. The will always controls. It is possible, through power, and the undue exercise of it, that the soul and the spiritual part of man are relegated to the background. It is not in the highest of places that spiritual development is the most common. It is a strange law of nature, that where power is given it is most generally abused. Let me ask you, on your honor as a gentleman, if you have every honestly sought to rise to the position of the ideal President?"

A very dignified look came over the face of the real President, and his reply astonished his cynical audience, who never had credited him before with possessing serious qualities. "Yes," said the President, "I have had high ambitions. I defy any man, however small, however petty, however selfish, to enter upon the great office of President of the United States without being lifted up by a sense of its tremendous responsibilities and requirements. He is in an attitude where the eye of every one is upon him. He has time-honored precedents behind him which govern his nearly every action. So high is his position, and so great the fame of those who have preceded him, that he is obliged to strive to satisfy an ambition which springs up in the heart of every incumbent of this office."

"But how did you proceed to try and meet that ambition, and to satisfy your ideal?"

At this, the look of pride and dignity left the President's face, as he replied :

"I must confess, that after that first emotion, when I rose to a height when I might have been entitled, perhaps, to meet even you, sir, upon a footing of equality, that I never had any more time left for anything but to walk in a treadmill, prepared by hoary precedent for every President. Sir, for the first six months of my occupancy of the office I was besieged through every waking moment, by a mad mob of office seekers. They came from every corner of the country, and cringed before me in every attitude of appeal."

"But why did you degrade the great office of President of the United States by giving up your time to the consideration of such petty matter? What would you think of the head of a great railroad corporation who spent ninety per cent. of his time discussing the merits of applications for the positions of brakemen on his road? What you have made to seem a bit of sacrifice was, after all, if you will pardon me the expression, an exercise of the quality of vanity, which loves to have in its own hands daily evidences of power, and a lack of executive capacity, in not being able to pass over to others three-quarters, if not nine-tenths, of the burdens which you so willingly and cheerfully carried."

The real President appeared to take no offense at this. He acted as if he were under the charm of a superior, whose criticisms were so kindly meant that they could not wound. He went on as if reciting a lesson in a class, or as if he were before a judge, making explanations. He said :

"After the first year I was able to escape the office-seekers, but then I became involved in a discussion with the Senate. The Senate objected to some of my appointments, and I put my foot down, to assert the rights of my great office, and to teach the Senate of the United States a lesson. I knew that the country would be with me, because the Senate, not being elected by the people, is never popular. And, so my time, up to the present, has been occupied with this controversy. Several senators have dared to make a personal war upon me, and I feel that I would be failing in my duty, in my high position, if I did not exhaust every power at my command to crush them, and to demonstrate the correctness of the principle underlying my conduct. I assure you, sir, there was nothing personal, no desiring to succeed for the sake of success, but simply a wish, upon my part, to prove that I was right, and being right, you, my perfect self, would not, surely, retreat one step."

"But were you right?"

"I followed the rules and precedents which have established the powers and prerogatives of my office."

"Is it your office?"

"No, not in the exact sense of the word ; still it is I, and it is I alone, who is called upon to decide what are

the duties of the President of the United States.   Who
can decide for me ? "

"But has it never occurred to you, that while you
may be abstractly correct, in defining such an issue,
yet, by your allowing that issue to become the predominating one of your administration, have you not
degraded the Government, and lowered your high
office to the plane of a petty personal issue ?   That
office is not yours.   It belongs to the people of the
United States.   You hold it in trust for them.   Your
manner of exercising those duties must be submitted
to your masters, the people, for their approval.   Are
you certain, in spite of your firm conviction, you, the
President of the United States, can now go before the
people on no other issue than the one you have established, who shall fill this or that office, and expect to
be continued in your office of trust ? "

A shadow of doubt came over the President's face.
He went over, in his politician's mind, the number of
delegates that were already pledged to him, but, before he could make any reply, his soul said : " That is
the mistake made by every professional politician.   I
was talking to you about a vote of confidence of the
people, and you immediately began to recapitulate, in
your own mind, the number of votes purchased by you
with offices for the coming convention.   What has that
to do with a vote of confidence ?   Is that in accordance
with your high ideas of the great office of the President of the United States seeking to try your individual claims before a packed jury ? "

The President still remained silent.   He sank into a

chair, and looked anxiously at the tall figure of his
double, who now leaned forward in his direction, and,
with an air of great earnestness, said : " Did it ever occur
to you, that in this great country, filled to overflowing
with multiplex interests, that a President, who is at the
head of the nation, should have his mind absolutely free
from all details, leaving it clear for the general sweep,
which embraces the whole country, so as to see all
questions relating to the public welfare, and to devote
his time to that which is most pressing and urging.
Have you ever thought of the general good of the
many? Don't answer me. I know there are some
very fine paragraphs in some of your messages, concerning the labor question, the value of arbitration,
and settling disputes between labor and capital, but
these suggestions of a moral character, relating to the
general welfare of the people themselves, were nothing
but the routine of approvals of the suggestions of
certain bureau chiefs in your department ; but, when
have you ever departed from the weary, time-worn path
and dared to make an original suggestion of a popular
kind? Have you ever ventured upon originality?
Have you not always trembled before those ancient
precedents, which are marshalled about the steps of
every President. Have you ever ventured to stand
upon the wrong square of the carpet during reception
hours, and have you not always occupied the particular
square which your predecessors have occupied on
similar occasions? Have you ever sought to free yourself from the environments of your situation—to
cast aside absurd etiquette, and to create, yourself, a

precedent? No, I am sure you never have. You
have been first steeped to the lips in the excitement of
a political campaign. Then, you have been drugged
with the vanity of power, and now you are consumed
by an ambition to be continued in that position of
power. You have never once forgotten self, and in the
end you will be forgotten, for no man can truly live
unless, during his life, he lives and works for others.
Your name can never be erased from the list of the
Presidents of the United States, but so long as you
are overwhelmed by selfish vanities you will pass on,
and the black letters, the symbols which go to compose
your name in the list, will represent less than nothing,
and will make no appeal to the grateful memory of any
one following after you."

CHAPTER XXIV.

THE PRESIDENT IS LEFT ALONE WITH CAPTAIN HARCOURT AND MYSELF.

Within a few moments after the close of the last scene, the guests, who had been assembled upon invitation by the President, departed. I was so interested in watching the President's face, and the dialogue between him and his double, that I cannot give a clear account of how the remainder of the guests received the signal to go. I merely state the result. Within five minutes after the departure of the guests, the double also disappeared, and the President was left alone with Captain Harcourt and myself.

The President now turned to Captain Harcourt and said :

" I have been strangely moved by the visions which you have placed before me, and, for the moment, I do not care to dispute their reality ; but I am, by no means, satisfied with what you have shown me. The conversation with my immortal soul has merely excited my curiosity, and I should like to continue the study of the subject, in so far as you may be able to help me. As I have been sitting here, many of the ideas which I had, when I first took the oath of office, have come back to me. Many of my old ambitions are revived. I believe that I am responsive to this better nature, which you have

invoked, and nothing is nearer to my heart than a
continuation of the conversation, and a further view of
the scenes representing the ideal President at his
work."

Said Captain Harcourt : " It has been my hope and
ambition to move you to the expression of such an
opinion. I can do nothing against your will, but I am
glad to see that you have, at least, been temporarily
impressed with the importance of the situation com-
manded by you and your capacity for doing a wrong,
as well as your ability to do good. The President of
the United States should be an example to all men.
He is the chief magistrate of a great nation. He lives
at the central point of power, and every eye should
be turned towards him for advice and encouragement.
He should always be above mere partisanship, and
ambition to serve merely personal ends. He should
be ready, at all times, to sacrifice his own interests for
those of the public. He should be an example of
honesty, of self-denial, and unselfishness to the whole
country. A President enjoying such a character, who
could resolutely put behind him all future personal
ambition, would command such loyal confidence that
he would be able to influence, to a great degree,
legislation, and, thereby, secure reforms not possible
to-day. Can you honestly say that you, yourself, have
any personal influence with Congress, the instrument of
the Government which regulates legislation ?"

To this the President replied : " I am frank to confess that my influence with Congress, to a certain extent, is negative. The messages which I send there

are generally pigeon-holed in the committees, and are never heard of unless I make a special effort, or special appeal, to prevail upon them to take them up. My opinions, unsupported by any attempt to back them by patronage, have really less weight than the average editorial opinion in the average newspaper."

" Do you know why this is so ?"

" I must confess that I have never looked closely into the reasons why. I know the dismal fact to be an unquestioned one."

" The reason why you have this lack of influence with Congress is because your attitude has always been a selfish one. You have never sent in a suggestion to Congress that has not had back of it the suspicion of advantage to your own fortunes. How can the country be interested in what concerns you, individually? You are, for the time being, a trustee ; and every time you prefer your own personal fortunes to those of the public, you are violating the conditions of the trust reposed in you. When you go to Congress with recommendations, you have to back them up with the full power of your patronage in order to make an impression ; but if you were to frankly and clearly renounce all personal ambition, and seek, merely, to advance the welfare of the public, then your suggestions would have weight. You would, then, be backed up by a public opinion, which, after all, is the controlling influence in all countries. The messages which you have sent to Congress have never once departed from the beaten track. I wonder if the time will ever come when a President of the United States will be able to send a short original message to Congress. What is there, in the environment of this office, which compels nearly every President to be profuse, verbose, and tautological? Some brief message of five hundred words, embracing a patriotic and unselfish idea, would make a most profound impression upon the country. The ideal President will ignore precedents; and his influence with the country will be measured, entirely, by his originality and his courage."

"I do not think that you fully measure the difficulties which stand in the way of any independent action upon the part of any President. A President is, naturally, conservative. The surroundings of his office make him so. He is an object of jealous regard by every one of the leaders in Congress, who, naturally, seek to occupy his place. Congress should be his natural ally. He can do nothing without its cordial support, yet he is never credited with honest or unselfish motives in that neighborhood. He has no friends there except those purchased by actual patronage. I think, in your criticism of me in the performance of my duties, that you have ignored the fact that a President has no real allies, and that he can only be successful in promoting some interest which enlists the selfish interests of the leaders in the other branches of the Government. A President never hears the truth about anything. He is surrounded by flatterers, and men whose interest it is to constantly misrepresent to him the facts. He never has the pleasure of hearing, except upon such an occasion

as this,"—and here he bowed to Captain Harcourt,—
"an honest criticism. Every one who seeks him has
some favor to ask. It is impossible for him to perform the simplest act of life without coming in contact with an army of self-seekers. He is hated by those
who are nearest him, because he can never satisfy
the desires of any one who comes to him ; for, you
must remember, that those who come to ask are never
satisfied, and that their demands are always beyond the
power of any President to grant. You have no idea,
unless you have a vision which sees everything, of the
trying situation which surrounds every President. He
really has more favors to grant than any potentate on
earth. As a necessary consequence, he is more be-
sought than any ruler of any nation. Looking at
matters seriously, in the light of what you have here
presented this evening, I can see that our Presidents
have altogether too much power ; and, if this question
of patronage and office distribution could be eliminated
from our national politics, we would have better
Presidents and more powerful administrations. It is
not natural, however, for any one to renounce power
once in his hands ; and every President who comes to
office finds it much more natural to use the weapons
in his hands, than to chivalrously strip himself and
enter the arena defenseless."

"Would it not be possible to imagine a condition of
affairs existing between Congress and the President,
which would be the opposite of the antagonistic one
which now exists?"

"Oh, I dare say. In that ideal future which you

have predicted, and pictured, men will be unselfish.
Presidents who are unselfish will not be considered
weak; and they will find the leaders in Congress ready
to support them in their suggestions, and not seek to
interpose the opposition dictated by their own personal ambitions; but, to-day, every one who rises to
prominence, in either House of Congress, has his eyes
firmly fixed upon the White House. Everything that
he does has a bearing upon his own personal ambition.
He, naturally, regards the incumbent of the White
House as his enemy, because the President, no matter
how self-sacrificing his private ambition, nearly always
seeks a renomination as a vote of confidence for his
administration. Every member and senator seeks to
obtain, from the President, everything that he can in
the way of offices to strengthen himself at home, and
he never even condescends to be grateful. He takes
what he can get as a matter of course, and is ready to
fight the President at the drop of the hat at the
slightest appearance of disfavor. More than this, the
President is made the scapegoat of the senators and
members. Through the dignity which surrounds his
office, his mouth is closed. The other side is always
heard. Nothing prevents a senator or member from
talking freely to the newspapers. Let me give you a
case in point, to show you the injustice with which a
President is treated, and how defenseless he is in influencing public opinion. Last year, a senator of the
United States sent to me an applicant for a prominent
office in his State. This applicant was the bearer of a
letter of most cordial endorsement from the senator in

question. He could not have written a more eulogistic letter for the most distinguished and worthy applicant for the highest honor. In fact, he left nothing to be said, after describing the virtues and ability of this gentleman, who, armed with such a letter, came to me, in all confidence, expecting the appointment. The next day after the reception of this glowing letter of endorsement, the senator himself called upon me. I said to him:

"'I have this appointment ready to be made out. Shall I have it sent to the Senate to-day?'

"He replied: 'What appointment?'

"I showed him his letter.

"'Oh,' he said, 'I have called to see you about that The fellow who brought you that letter is a very strong man in my State. He has a big political pull, and I want to keep on his right side; but I hate him like the devil, and I would not have you appoint him for anything. So far as that letter is concerned, you may stick it in the waste basket.'

"Well, you know, that is politics, and so I did not feel like saying very much; but, about nine months after, I received a letter from this same applicant for office, who enclosed to me a letter from the senator. The applicant said:

"'Mr. President, I think I have been very hardly treated. I came to you with an application for an office, endorsed by the most powerful senator in the country. I am a member of the State Central Committee, and, I think, my position entitles me to some consideration; yet, I have been ignored, and have received no consideration. I respectfully submit to you the enclosed letter from the senator in question, showing what he thinks of my treatment.'

"And what do you think this senator, who was the very man who had asked me, verbally, not to appoint this man, wrote? He had the hardihood to address a letter, himself, to this applicant, which was filled with indignation from beginning to end. He said, in so many words: 'I have labored in vain with the President. I have written the strongest letters, as you know, and I have made the most vigorous appeal. The President is a vain, selfish man, who seeks only his own advancement. He is thoroughly discredited now by his party, and his action in your case is only a fair sample of what he has done in other directions.' Do you know, the very morning that I received this letter the senator called upon me to ask me to help him secure his re-election by giving him a few of the offices in his State. He was as calm, and as gentle and deprecating in his demand, as if he were my most sincere and loyal supporter; and yet I had that letter from him in my own desk, and it was a great piece of self-denial upon my part not to take it out and read it to him."

"What you have said," said Captain Harcourt, "after all, has a great bearing upon what I have sought to demonstrate. So long as the national issues are personal and selfish, so long as the thought of personal advancement controls, there will be treachery and personal deception; but the moment a President takes upon himself an attitude of unselfishness, and is persistent, throughout his administration, in advancing ideas which are solely to benefit the country, then, and then only, will he receive the honest support to which he is entitled. Let him forever banish from his mind the thought whether he is to be re-elected or not; let him do his whole duty in the history of the march of progress in this country. There have been one or two shining examples who have approached to the ideal in their unselfishness. These were Washington and Lincoln. Look at the places which they now occupy in history; compare their fame with the fame of those who are merely place-seekers. But, permit me to call your attention to one more great scheme in the ideal Government, and this will, perhaps, impress more upon you what I wish to convey than any mere succession of words and phrases."

CHAPTER XXV.

THE PRESIDENT ON TRIAL IN THE FORUM—THE CHARGES PRESENTED, AND HIS FINAL ACQUITTAL.

The last scene in the series, presented to the attention of the President, was the most important, and possessed, for me, the greatest interest. It came as a climax to the suggestive pictures of the night. It embraced more positive action, and showed up in clearer lines. In the few moments which preceded its presentation, the President sat buried in profound thought. Whether it was his wish to be left alone or not, I do not know, but before the closing scene was thrown upon the ideal screen of Captain Harcourt, the guests, without saying farewell, had withdrawn, one by one, from the room. This I did not notice until the grey clouds, which formed in advance of every picture, had swirled through the room and were gone. Then I observed that the President was alone with Captain Harcourt and myself.

As the veil parted for the last time, there stood out a wonderful picture, shining clear in a soft, bright light of an early October day in Washington. In the center of the scene I recognized the neighborhood as the Heights to the northwest of Georgetown, just beyond Rock Creek Park, a point of view which commands the beautiful Valley of the Potomac, from the

Three Sisters, at the north, to the far-away hills of Maryland, to the south. The Forum, which occupied the highest point, was a great circular building, built upon the lines of the Coliseum at Rome. It had the same solid, circling stone seats, reaching up in the form of easily mounted *gradins*, to a height which could easily accommodate one hundred thousand people. These seats were arranged about an open space, which was floored in marble, and covered with the paraphernalia of a court. I only looked for a moment at the interior. It was the exterior of the building that first interested me. To the right and left of this circular arena were great buildings, in architectural keeping with the character of the central building. They were simple and massive, abounding in stately portal archways, and flanked by terraces, upon which stood beautiful statues, and graceful ornaments in iron, setting off the brilliant work of skilled landscape gardeners. The crest upon which these buildings were placed was approached by a broad, stately roadway, flanked by statues and public buildings. Up this roadway I saw coming a great host of people. At their head was a convoy of heralds, dressed in robes of dark purple. The notes of the march, sounded by them, were in a minor key, sorrowful in their sweetness. There was no form to the moving hosts; there was no attempt to march rank by rank; there was not a carriage visible in the throng, save the three or four which followed directly after the heralds. The carriages were filled with grave and honest-looking men, ten in number.

The President spoke : " Who are these men ? What is the meaning of this ceremony ? "

There was an accent of trouble in his voice as he asked these questions. He seemed to have a premonition that the scene related to him personally. The answer was : " Those men compose the Court of Honor ; they are now on the way to the Forum to conduct a great and important trial."

" The trial of an official ? "

" Yes, the trial of an official."

" He must be high in station to call forth such a concourse of people ? "

" Yes, he is the highest of all. He is the President of the United States."

" But you are portraying an ideal condition. How could charges be made against an ideal person ? "

" On this earth the absolute ideal is never reached. I can only show you approximately ideal conditions, but the picture, which I show you here, is not even an attempt to present wholly ideal conditions. I wish to show you, representing the school of politics at the present time, on trial before a Court of Honor, the ideal tribunal for the presentation of public grievances against the chief magistrate."

The President was startled. He said : " Will it be really I who will be on trial there ? "

" Yes, in so far as the art of the ideal world can reach, you will be represented there. Do you fear such a trial ? "

The President made no answer. He studied, curiously, the moving hosts, which now began to approach the portals of the Forum. Suddenly, he said : " Why are the people so sorrowful and melancholy? Why do the heralds play such lugubrious music?"

" The people are sad, because they feel that it is a grievous thing when the chief of any nation apparently fails in his duty, and that what reflects upon him indirectly reflects upon all. If you can come forth from that Court of Honor spotless, and free from all charges, you will witness, in that picture, such a scene of joy, and hear such melodies of gaiety, as will charm your soul. But, if the verdict is against you, the gloom will only deepen, and the ideal nation will not be able to hold up its head again until the condemned President has placed his resignation in the hands of the Court of Honor, and has gone forth, as a private citizen, to seek, through the loving performance of some humbler duty, forgiveness for his past acts."

The scene now changed to the interior of the Forum. The picture became so real that we entered into actual participation in its incidents. The President was no longer in the White House. He was seated in one of the waiting rooms, on the same floor with the circular space devoted to the officials of the court, at the foot of the *gradins*. Captain Harcourt and I occupied a seat in the front ranks of the lower tier, where we could watch every movement of the actors in this magnificent scene. I know of no more splendid, moving sight than a great gathering of refined, intelligent and handsomely dressed people. Upon the tier which rose above round about us, there was a succession of handsome faces, athletic and gracefully formed figures, clothed in soft and artistic colors, which, in the robes of the ladies, flashed into hues of intense brilliancy, while, with the men, the key of the colors, as now, ran to more sombre tones. The Forum, like the Coliseum, was open at the top ; a great crimson awning, caught at the center upon an arch of steel, and sustained by lines of steel, radiating like the spokes of a wheel from the center, protected the assembly from the concentrated light of the mid-day sun. The awning whipped and snapped, moving like a brilliant sea of color, flashing its warmth below upon the white robes and the rich colors of the many-hued garments of this ideal populace.

My attention, which followed in lazy delight, for a moment, the picture of this great audience, now suddenly turned to the arena. The heralds entered first and sounded their bugles, three notes only; then came in the various dignitaries of the court, clad in white silk robes and black skull caps. Then came the members of the Court of Honor, in black silk robes and red skull caps.

These gentlemen took their seats, the audience rising as they entered. The fluttering of the robes, the uprising and down-sitting of the audience made a most impressive reception to the entrance of the judges.

A moment later, the bugles again sounded, and played a formal, ceremonious march. The audience now rose again, and in the midst of a profound silence, which followed the end of the heralds' notes, there entered the President of the United States. It was the President, as I had seen him at the White House.

There he had learned a certain dignity and stoicism, which now stood him well as he faced this court. He entered with proud dignity, walked easily to the great chair placed at his disposal at a table on the right, and then appeared to be absorbed in a paper which was handed to him, and which, I soon learned, contained the charges to be made against him. On the opposite side of the table there were seats placed for the Cabinet advisers, who came in directly after him. They appeared to be ill at ease and unhappy, and caught eagerly at the copy of the charges, which was handed to each of them by pages, who flew about the Court, bringing in documents and books, and attending to the wants of the grave officials who were charged with the prosecution and the defense before this High Court.

The President of the court now rose and directed one of the heralds to read the charges. The acoustic properties of this Forum were arranged with such skillful art that the lowest note of the herald's voice was heard by the the most distantly placed in the audience. These charges, which I noted at the time, were brief. As the herald read them, they were as follows:

Charge 1. *Neglect of the public welfare.*

SPECIFICATION 1. That he, the President, has never submitted to Congress a single measure in the interest of the public, and that he has been governed in all his suggestions by personal and partisan influences.

SPECIFICATION 2. That he, the President, has taken

to himself the appointment of all the federal officials in the United States, for the purpose of advancing his own selfish ends; and that, under a pretense of guarding the public welfare, he has left himself no leisure for consideration of public questions.

SPECIFICATION 3. That he, the President, has so cultivated his vanity, through personal contemplation of his own merits, that he has grown to think that he is, himself, the law, constitution and the country combined, and that any advice, or suggestion, from any human being, relating to his personal conduct, is an insult and a reflection upon his rights.

SPECIFICATION 4. That he, the President of the United States, has forgotten that he has been called upon to fulfil a trust extended to him by the people, and that he has come to regard the office as one personal to himself, and that the powers given to that office are to be used only for the advancement of his own personal ambitions.

SPECIFICATION 5. That he, the President, has permitted his friends to so surround him with adulation and gross flattery, that he has, thereby, closed to his intelligence all the channels through which intelligence and truth might be able to reach him.

SPECIFICATION 6. That he, the President of the United States, has built up, in his own mind, an image of himself, which he has labeled "a man of destiny," and which he worships as his only God.

The President's face was a very curious study during

the reading of these charges. He turned and glared at
Captain Harcourt, then came back to himself, and I saw
him furtively pinching the interior of his palm, as if
to assure himself whether this was a dream or a reality.
But, as he was thus engaged, the note of the heralds again
rang out, and then a sonorous voice sounded: "Who
appears to accuse this man?" There now appeared,
in the arena, representatives of all classes, and I observed that the humblest came first. In the front
rank there stood a workman, hollow-eyed and hungry.
He was the first to speak. He said: "I accuse this
man. When he came into office the country was rich
and prosperous. The laws for the protection of the
humblest were wise and well administered. I had
plenty of work, and my family was well and clothed.
Since he has come into office all this has been changed.
His personal, selfish and mad ambition has upset the
comfort and peace of the country. He, blinded by his
position, deaf to everything but the flattery of syco-
phants, ignores the cries of the starving, and talks of
the object lesson which he is giving to the country."
The cruel picture of the man's sufferings, described in
pathetic phrases and emphatic gestures, were most
carefully noted down by the scribes of this court; for,
it must be remembered, in this ideal court, the highest
could be accused by the humblest, and that no man
could be so high and proudly placed that he could not
be summoned to the defense of charges made by the
poorest and the weakest.

After the workmen, came the representatives of the
trade and industries that had been crushed by the

selfish, partisan folly of a President, who had sought to build up and please one section of the country, and to ignore a great commercial life and movement of the nation, whose destinies he had held in his hands at such a critical period.

It was painful to watch this accumulation of eloquent denunciation, ranging from the workmen to the great capitalists, who had, in this court, rights placing them on an equality with the poor.

The President of the United States was not overcome by these charges. In fact, no one had ever questioned his courage. The longer the accusations, the more energetic and resentful became his attitude. In this court, the accused spoke last. During the day, the specifications were sustained by eloquent argument, and by the hearing of witnesses, according to the usual forms of law. The line of argument for the prosecution related to the general charge of neglect of the public welfare.

There was a great interest when the President rose to reply. Several of his Cabinet officers desired to speak in his defense, but he forbade them with a contemptuous glance. He said: "This is my case. These charges are made against me, and I alone will answer them." The President now adroitly shifted the whole ground by saying: "It's not very clear yet, to my mind, how I came to be before this court at all. This court, as I understand it, is an ideal one, and represents an age to which I do not belong. I submit, in the first place, that it is not fair or just that an unideal person, surrounded by conditions anything but ideal, should be tried before such a court. If I have not always followed the highest line of conduct in my office, it is because I have found myself alone. A man is, at best, limited in his capacity and ability to do; and in the political world, in which I have moved, and where I have built my fortunes, I do not know of a single influence which is high or lofty. The influences in the political world are selfish. The leaders of both parties seek only their personal ends. Let me reach to the right or the left for support, and I cannot find it unless I am ready to sacrifice my personal inclinations, and to offer bribes, in the shape of place and power. I take the world as I found it. I have sought to do the best that I could within the lines that surrounded me, and I have never, for a moment, supposed that my line of action approached the semblance of the ideal."

The speech of the President continued for nearly an hour. It was bitter, caustic in its denunciation of men and things, and a cruel, running criticism upon the injustice of trying an unideal character in a court controlled by ideal conditions. So adroit and so forcefully did he present this view, that, at the close of his talk, the Court of Honor rose and submitted a judgment that, in all essential points, the charges had been sustained, but that the main line of the defense submitted by the President was one that could not be ignored. He had lived up to the conditions which had surrounded him at the time of his being brought to trial. If he had been a stronger man, he might have surmounted them. More than this—he was ignorant. His eyes were closed to the advantages of unselfishness, and, while technically guilty, equity demanded that he should be acquitted.

This judgment was repeated again and again, with pauses for voices of disapproval from those present; but not a single " No " was heard, and the thundering " Aye! " that came with the affirmation had in it a note of pity for the blind, uncivilized man who had maintained himself so gallantly before this bar of high civilization.

The scene suddenly disappeared, and I now saw the President seated again in his chair in the library at the White House. It was four o'clock in the morning. There was a satirical look on his face, as he turned to Captain Harcourt. He said: "Say, you are not such a bad fellow, and you understand your business very well. I don't exactly see how you produce all these things. I suppose if I did I would not care. I consider your system highly impracticable, although amusing as a spectacular performance. You may change the world over, by a systematic presentation of ideal possibilities; but I fancy that many, many centuries will pass before the first shadow of your ideal pictures will take upon themselves the form of a reality. However, you have ability, and, as you have friends, if you get the proper endorsements, I will see that you have any good appointment—almost any you would like in the foreign service. I would not have you think that I am inappreciative of the influence you possess, or unmindful of the influence of your friends."

" I am very much obliged to you," said Captain Harcourt, "for your kind thoughtfulness; but what you propose I could not accept." With this he bowed, and we walked out of the White House, crossing Lafayette Park in the early grey of the morning. Two hours later he left Washington. I was to follow him, after I had prepared the record of the first work of his society in Washington. This chapter concludes my report. To-morrow I shall set off for the Island of Nolos, to look farther into the theories of Captain Harcourt and Doctor Longman.

[THE END.]